———————— ★ ————————

"Mom, please tell me what happened."

This was the second time I'd pressed her since leaving Eagle's Cliff. She'd waved away my first attempt over mugs of Earl Grey at the Laughing Whitefish Cafe—a popular diner that overlooks Apostle Bay's iron-ore dock. She'd tried hiding her tears when I asked by pretending to study the rail cars dumping iron pellets into a freighter. Red ore dust had smoked out of the ship's hold, creating a temporary haze over the lake.

Instead of answering at the restaurant, she'd whispered, "I can't." Then she wiped her eyes and struck up a "How's-the-weather?" conversation with a friend who walked by our table.

The weeping had me puzzled and a bit worried. I can't recall a single teary-eyed moment in Mom's past, including Dad's passing. I'd been the emotional wreck at that event. Mom was her archetypal stoic self.

"The chief said you found her body."

A sniffle.

"Did you see her fall? Is it someone you know? C'mon, Mom. You have to talk about it."

She patted my arm. "I can't."

———————— ★ ————————

MATTHEW WILLIAMS

SUPERIOR DEATH

TORONTO • NEW YORK • LONDON
AMSTERDAM • PARIS • SYDNEY • HAMBURG
STOCKHOLM • ATHENS • TOKYO • MILAN
MADRID • WARSAW • BUDAPEST • AUCKLAND

This work is dedicated to Suzanne
for her unconditional love, support, friendship
and encouragement.

Recycling programs
for this product may
not exist in your area.

SUPERIOR DEATH

A Worldwide Mystery/August 2013

First published by Avalon Books

ISBN-13: 978-0-373-26861-0

Printed in U.S.A.

ONE

RUDY CLARK WAS HARD TO MISS, strutting around the room like a bantam rooster convinced of his own beauty and importance. Knocking this pompous jerk down a notch would be sweet.

Maybe next time he'd return my calls.

I leaned further around the door to see who of our town's so-called luminaries were at this morning's Rotary breakfast, and caught a whiff of eggs and sausage. Six men and three women ignored Clark, intent on lining their arteries with plaque. A waitress delivered more food. A waiter refilled coffee mugs.

In a word: Snooz-o-rama. I figured these people could use a little excitement to jump start their day.

I checked my watch: twenty-five minutes to deadline.

Clark, our county prosecutor, was still squawking and striding around the room on his ever-present platform shoes. He brushed against the waitress as he passed and smirked while asking her pardon. I watched her consider shoving a load of bacon into his artificially tanned face.

Oblivious to her indignation, Clark snatched a bacon slice from the platter and dropped into the seat beside… oh, man, beside the chief.

Dale Weathers, our irascible police chief and also my

godfather, looked crankier than usual this morning. I was sure he wanted to slap Clark upside the head. How he tolerated the man's chummy pat on the back without flinching was beyond me, especially after the prosecutor refused to support his detectives earlier this week.

Despite his scowl, however, my godfather is a company man to the core. He wouldn't publicly air his opinion of Clark. Too bad, because I'd give a week's pay to see the head slap, or maybe see him pretend to greet Clark and then crush the prosecutor's hand in his monster grip until... Well, wishful thinking.

For my plan to work, though, I had to get rid of the chief. Tough as it was to swallow, the prosecutor was a law-enforcement official who, the chief would say, was due our respect. He would no doubt cut me off when I cornered Clark and growl his usual "Show some manners, Vince."

I pulled back into the hotel corridor and checked my watch again. Deadline loomed. A couple of tourists hoarding donuts from the continental breakfast walked by and I pretended to study the cheesy wildflower prints on the wall. Time for Plan B: Call the front desk and have them page the chief.

I pulled out my cell phone, leaned back into the room for a second look and nearly got an imprint of the chief's badge on my nose.

"Hey, Chief. What's the hurry?"

He grunted and pushed past, distracted by whatever mission he was on. I shrugged, said a brief prayer that he was heading further than the restroom down the hall and stepped through the door. The chief's seat was still warm when I parked in it and lay my recorder on the table.

"That chair's taken," Rudy Clark said.

"Hello to you, too, Rudy." I pushed the record button. "Mr. Prosecutor, how is it that—"

Clark reached over and pushed the stop button. "Call my office and make an appointment."

I pressed the record button again and slid the machine out of his reach. "I have. Been there, too. You're dodging me, Rudy. Why didn't you authorize the possession charge against that kid this week? You cracked the whip on his classmates—why not him? The cops tell me the evidence is solid, that it's a stronger case than their previous arrests, and those all resulted in convictions."

"Who told you that?"

"Was there a problem with the arrest?"

"This conversation is over," Clark said, his voice rising like it always does when he drives home a point in court. The Rotarians had stopped eating to watch us. Clark played to them. "I won't let your tabloid-style journalism ruin our breakfast. Or interrupt the important work of this community organization."

"Sure, Mr. Prosecutor, I just wanted to give you a chance to explain why, out of all the recent drug arrests, the only kid to walk is also the son of your campaign treasurer. The story runs in today's edition. Deadline is now fifteen minutes. Enjoy your scrambled eggs."

I smiled at the other Rotarians as I stood, noticing a few were hiding their own grins.

"Please," I said, taking a bow, "continue with your important work."

My cell phone chirped when I reached the corridor and I flipped it open.

"Hello."

"Vince." It was the chief's no-nonsense growl. I heard a siren wailing in the background. "Get your tail down to Eagle's Cliff."

"No time, Chief. I'm on deadline."

"Not anymore. We're fishing a woman's body out of the lake."

"A drowning? Or did another tourist take an unplanned dive over the edge?"

"This isn't an interview. Your mother's here, and she found the body."

TWO

I'M NOT TOO KEEN on seeing dead people—at this point in my life the only body I've seen up close was my father's, and that was enough for a while.

No worries about that here, though. When I ducked under the police tape cordoning off a section of Eagle's Cliff and peered over the edge, the dead woman was some seventy-five feet below me. She rested in a blaze-orange Zodiac, her legs sticking out from a silvery blanket that covered her torso and face. The boat rocked in a light swell. Two U.S. Coast Guard ensigns talked with a diver hanging on the edge of their craft. Lake Superior was teal; chunks of broken cliff were visible on the bottom another twenty-five feet down.

I watched the diver peel back his hood, knowing I'd see the black curls of Detective Captain Gordon Greenleaf, my high-school bud and the only certified scuba diver on the force. I raised my camera, focused the telephoto lens and snapped pictures of Greenleaf talking with the ensigns while the body lay between them. I knew the shots weren't great from that angle, but I could zoom in on the body and caught one picture of an ensign adjusting the sheet that covered her. It would have to do.

"Hey. What do you think you're doing?"

I looked back, didn't recognize the guy jogging toward me, then checked the view screen on my camera to see how the shots looked.

"Give me the camera."

The guy—bald, bad suit, snarling face—was twenty feet away and still coming at me. I turned off the camera and moved away from the edge, circling to keep a little distance between us. That's when I noticed the badge clipped to his belt and radio in his left hand, and realized this must be the city's new detective. Gordon had described the new guy as "kind of a cowboy."

"I'm Vince Marshall with the *Chronicle*," I said, still keeping some distance. "The chief called me."

"I don't think so," the cop said. "Don't you know what that yellow tape back there means, buddy? It means I'm confiscating that camera and kicking you outta here."

He pointed the radio at me like it was his weapon. "I'm not kidding," I said, nodding at his radio and feeling like I should raise my hands. "Check with the chief."

"Right—"

A burst of static, then the chief's voice: "Send him over to me, Archie."

The cop glared, raised the radio and said, "I can handle it. He's just a lousy reporter."

"Send him over."

The cop's head and neck flushed and he mumbled a string of curses before turning to look along the cliff. I raised a hand to block the sun and followed his gaze to the silhouette of two people leaning together some eighty feet away. Before Cowboy Cop had a chance to reconsider, I made a wide berth and scrambled toward the chief and my mom.

EAGLE'S CLIFF IS A PENINSULA reaching a half mile into Lake Superior. I think of it as a crooked finger of granite, beckoning ore freighters to come kiss its dizzying, striated cliffs.

Most of the peninsula is green during summer, covered by cedar, striped maple, red pine and other hardy plants that eke out a tenuous existence. But the last fifty yards, the point, is an exposed shelf of black-stained igneous rock—the remnant of a billion-year-old lava flow, thrust upward by the earth and scoured by eons of glaciers and Lake Superior storms.

The place is a tourist magnet, for the view of Lake Superior as well as the eagle's nest visible in a towering red pine when your back is to the lake. It's also a favorite year-round hangout for locals. And it's a continuous source of debate for our city council members, who can't agree on whether to erect a safety rail at the cliff's edge or keep defending lawsuits from the few fools—often inebriated—who fall. If they're lucky fools, rescue workers will pull them from the wicked-cold water with only twisted arms, broken legs and hypothermia.

Every summer at least one person is not that lucky.

I PICKED MY WAY OVER cracks and bare rock toward the couple. Mom leaned against the chief, her broad back and shoulders heaving. A few yards short of them, her watercolor kit lay askew on the ground. I stepped over a broken easel leg.

"Mom?"

She pushed away from the chief and swiped tears from her face. Mom's a tall, athletic Norwegian-American, and she grabbed me, pinning my arms so I couldn't return her hug.

I caught the chief's eye and nodded back toward the cliff. "Who is she?"

"That's not your concern. Take your mother home and stay with her."

He'd said those same words six years ago, in dad's room at St. Mark's Hospital, the night dad died.

"C'mon, Mom," I said. "Where's your car?"

"I'll have an officer bring it later," Weathers said, jingling keys he'd already confiscated. "You take her home. And, Vince, don't stop at the *Chronicle* on your way. They can get by without you today."

The chief reached forward, hesitated, then patted Mom on the back. "I'll check on you this afternoon, Loretta," he said. Then he walked past us toward the cliff, speaking into his radio.

Mom released me, planted a kiss on my forehead, then bent to pack up her painting kit. I squatted, picked up the easel and examined the broken leg.

"What happened to this?"

"Couldn't hold my weight, I guess."

I waited for her to say more, but she snapped the kit closed and stood.

"What were you working on?" I asked. "Another project for art class?"

"We're supposed to do sunsets, but I'm not that productive in the evening, so I do the sunrise." Mom forced a laugh. "The teacher can't tell the difference."

I put an arm around her and pulled her close. "Dad would have called that a creative interpretation of the teacher's instructions."

We started toward the car. For a moment the weathered rock shifted to pavement and I recalled that night at St. Mark's, walking to the car, my arm around Mom—the night that brought me back to Apostle Bay.

I blinked away the past and asked, "Are you going to tell me what happened?"

She shook her head.

In the gravel parking lot, I guided Mom around a white camper, the back-of-the-pickup-truck type. Someone had painted a red, twirling cowgirl on its side.

The passenger door of my rusty Bronco screeched a protest as Mom pulled it open and climbed in. I stowed her kit in the back, dropped my camera on the seat and opened my cell phone.

"I'm going to call Deb and tell her not to bring Glory today," I said. "She can rearrange her schedule."

"Don't you dare. If there's ever been a day I needed my granddaughter's smiling face, it's today."

"Mom—"

"And don't coddle me." Mom wagged her finger at me. It looked oddly familiar and I realized where I'd seen the gesture: Two nights earlier my toddler daughter,

Glory, disagreeing with her bedtime, had struck the same pose. "I don't care what the chief said. I only get Glory two days a week, and I'm not giving her up."

"Okay, but first I'll call Deb and tell her we'll be late. We're stopping by the Laughing Whitefish for a cup of tea. Just to warm our hands if nothing else. After that we'll get Glory."

I pressed the speed dial for home. A man answered after the third ring. I looked at the phone to make sure I'd dialed correctly.

"Hello?" the man said again.

"Who's this?"

"It's Tony. Is that you, Vince?"

"Why are you answering my phone?"

"Deb is changing Glory's diaper. She asked me to grab it. Something wrong?"

Yeah, you're at my house.

"Hang on, Vince. Here she is."

"Hi," Deb said. She was out of breath.

"What's up with Wittmer?"

"What do you mean?"

"I mean, is he our new answering service?"

"We're getting ready for tonight's meeting. You didn't forget that, did you?" My wife had that "You've obviously not been paying attention" tone in her voice. "We have another bargaining session. You're supposed to get Glory from your mom's house after work."

"That's why I called." I explained the situation. "Mom insists she's fine, but I want to spend a little time with her first. We'll come get Glory in about an hour."

"Who died?"

I moved toward the Bronco's rear and lowered my voice. "No clue. The chief sent me away with a lecture about taking care of Mom and not going to work. Something seems strange. Mom's not acting like her normal self. The chief is more tight-lipped than usual."

"If you hear anything, let me know," Deb said.

"Yeah, see you in a few."

"I love you, Vince."

"Thanks." I felt strange not telling her I loved her, too, and a little bit petty, but this Tony guy hanging around so much was starting to annoy me.

I dialed the *Chronicle* and connected with Gina Holt. Gina is the paper's editorial clerk, office manager, obit writer, sometimes gossip columnist and lead skeptic. Nothing unsettles Gina.

"I need a big favor, Gina."

"When don't you?" she said with her usual dose of sarcasm. "Where are you anyway? Rudy Clark was here screaming all kinds of crazy stuff when I told him you hadn't arrived. I thought he was going to bust an artery."

"Will you please meet me outside the building in five minutes? I have photos of a dead body. You'll need the camera ASAP to get it on the page."

"Anyone we know?"

"I don't know."

"You're not writing the story?"

"Can't. Transfer me to the boss and I'll give him the details."

"Okay," she said with an exaggerated sigh. I knew

she'd expect some kind of payback for this. "I want a cigarette anyway. Five minutes, buster. You'd better be there."

THREE

"MOM, PLEASE TELL ME what happened."

This was the second time I'd pressed her since leaving Eagle's Cliff. She'd waved away my first attempt over mugs of Earl Grey at the Laughing Whitefish Cafe— a popular diner that overlooks Apostle Bay's iron-ore dock. She'd tried hiding her tears when I asked by pretending to study the rail cars dumping iron pellets into a freighter. Red ore dust had smoked out of the ship's hold, creating a temporary haze over the lake.

Instead of answering at the restaurant, she'd whispered "I can't." Then she wiped her eyes and struck up a "How's the weather?" conversation with a friend who walked by our table.

The weeping had me puzzled and a bit worried. I can't recall a single teary-eyed moment in Mom's past, including dad's passing. I'd been the emotional wreck at that event. Mom was her archetypal stoic self.

Now, as my Bronco's tires left pavement and crunched onto our gravel drive, I took another shot at prying some information from her.

"The chief said you found her body."

A sniffle.

"Did you see her fall? Is it someone you know? C'mon, Mom. You have to talk about it."

She patted my arm. "I can't. Just forget it. I'm fine."

She opened the door as we stopped at the drive's end, the ungreased hinge protesting again. I slipped the gear into Park and turned toward her.

"Look, Mom, if you were fine you wouldn't—"

She slammed the door on me.

GLORY, MY YEAR-AND-A-HALF-OLD daughter, charged off the porch and across the lawn toward us. I squatted to her level, held out my arms and watched this miniature replica of my wife—inquisitive dark eyes, midnight-black hair, a petite, upturned nose and a mischievous grin—come running.

That grin was a dare, a challenge to any type of authority. On Deb it had captured my heart in sophomore English lit class the first time we'd met—she was the confident, brazen woman who'd ruined the grading curve; I was the guy dozing in the back row because I'd pulled an all-nighter at the campus newspaper. These days, when Glory flashed it after sticking pebbles up her nose or flipping her dinner plate, the grin seemed less endearing.

Glory didn't inherit any of my looks, but Deb said our daughter had clearly gotten my stubborn streak.

The little whippersnapper swerved past my outstretched arms and into Mom's embrace. Deb followed and hugged Mom, too.

"How are you doing, Loretta?" Deb asked.

"Glor-ee-us," said Mom, her usual carefree play on Glory's name sounding forced. She lifted Glory to her hip and kissed her forehead.

"Why don't you stay for lunch?" Deb asked.

"A good idea," I added.

"Quit worrying about me. You're both worse than the chief."

Glory squirmed to the ground and tugged Mom's leg.

"House," she said in her high-pitched voice. Mom shrugged, gave a weak smile and followed her across the lawn.

"Your mom's been crying," Deb whispered. "I didn't know she could."

"She's been that way since I found her at Eagle's Cliff."

"Do you know what happened yet?"

"She won't say. All the chief told me was that Mom discovered the body."

"That must have been a shock."

"Yeah, maybe. But the water's a long way down. If she saw someone floating, she probably couldn't even tell if it was a man or a woman, much less recognize the person."

"Are you sure she's okay watching Glory?"

"Sure. Glory will keep her mind off of whatever is upsetting her."

We started toward the house, a one-story bungalow that was my family's summer camp until Deb and I moved here from Grand Rapids after Dad's death—a move that had set back both of our careers, but one that was worth it to be near Mom and back in Michigan's Upper Peninsula. Mom had the place insulated and a furnace installed when she learned we were moving north.

The place is tiny for a family—two bedrooms, living room and eat-in kitchen. But there are too many good memories of sandcastles and beach bonfires for me to give it up. And too many memories of Dad, inept at skipping rocks but trying to teach me anyway. We'd laugh at his clunkers 'til our cheeks hurt.

Deb puts up with cramped quarters, I think, because she feels some sort of kinship with the wild seasonal storms that whip Superior into a froth and send the behemoth ore freighters fleeing to protected harbors. Sometimes, when a particularly nasty blow wakes Glory from sleep, I know I'll find Deb standing at the kitchen window, nursing Glory and staring at the thundering surf.

INSIDE I POURED lemonade and brewed coffee while Deb set out sandwich fixings. Glory and Mom played in the living room.

"When you stopped into the station this morning, did Gordon tell you they arrested another of our students?" she asked. "It was drugs again."

"All Gordon and I talked about was how bad his coffee tastes." I noticed her annoyed expression and added, "Sorry. Yep, he told me. With everything going on this morning, I haven't looked into it yet."

"I know the boy pretty well. He was in my biology class."

I'd learned about the arrest during my daily visit to

city hall, where I checked the overnight dispatch log and then sipped a mug of Greenleaf's notorious coffee, bought in bulk from some web site and brewed through a brown paper towel. Our morning coffee klatch is mostly a gossip session, since there's rarely police business to discuss. The prevalent crimes in Apostle Bay are drunk driving and domestic violence, and a large segment of the town's 15,000 blue-collar folk don't consider these transgressions.

"He's a good kid," she continued. "Something's not right. I'd bet he wouldn't even know where to buy pot or how to roll a joint if he did."

"I guess you'd lose that wager. Hope his parents contributed to Rudy Clark's campaign."

Deb rolled her brown eyes, then said, "I hear he's claiming the stuff was planted on him."

"C'mon, Deb. Every kid says that."

"I hope this time it's true."

I moved to the window, looked at the boulder-strewn shoreline outside. Gulls wheeled over the lake, dipping at times into the swell. Dune grass swayed on the beach's edge.

Including yesterday's bust, police had nabbed eight local teens with pot during the last month—that's a major epidemic for Apostle Bay. The first arrest came back in mid-July, the week of my birthday. That was a disaster. I'd heard about it on the scanner while making a short trip to the corner store for ice to refill the cooler and, well, let's just say I lost track of time chasing the story, the pop and beer got warm, everyone went home.

Deb was hot about it for a week.

"What about the other kids arrested this summer?" I asked. "Do you know them?"

"Yeah. They're driven, topnotch kids, not the kind to make a mistake like this."

"Maybe one of them brought a stash back from summer vacation. Smart kids experiment, too. I'll ask around."

"By the way, we still need to find daycare for Glory. I'm full-time in the classroom next week—that is, if we settle the contract. That's looking like a big *if* right now."

"What about Mom?"

"No," whispered Deb. "We've already discussed that. I love Loretta. Two days a week is great. But every day is not fair to her or to Glory. Glory needs exposure to other children."

"Mama?"

We both turned toward the hallway. Glory and Mom stood watching us.

"Hi, Morning Glory," Deb said. "Are you and Nana ready for lunch?"

FOUR

PLAIN AND SIMPLE: Lou Kendricks came to Apostle Bay to die. Most of the time, I'm glad it didn't work out as he'd planned.

A couple of years back, a faulty ticker ended Lou's thirty-five years at the *Chicago Herald*. The heart attack came on a Monday, a slow news day, the type of day that I'm sure irked Lou, who was then managing editor. In this case a lack of news saved his life. A half-hour before deadline, the city editor went for coffee and noticed Lou splayed face down on his keyboard. The city editor's fast response saved Kendricks from brain damage, according to the cardiologist. Kendricks had supposedly replied, "The kid's work is so bad it shriveled most of my gray matter years ago anyway."

Soon after he left the hospital, Lou took early retirement, or he was pushed out the door. It depended on his mood when telling the story. Either way, the kid who ruined his gray cells had moved into his desk.

I knew enough about Lou's past and why he came north to liken his near-death experience to the *Chronicle*'s. We were a second-rate paper with ancient equipment when our owner went AWOL two years ago. Most employees were only going through the motions—when they bothered showing up. Deb was pregnant and I was mass mailing resumes across Michigan and Wisconsin.

Lou, meanwhile, moved to a lakefront home twenty miles west of town that he'd bought as a retirement place—just like Lou to go in the opposite direction of his peers, who spend their golden years in sun-filled southern communities.

Instead of croaking as planned, he got bored. Our beleaguered newspaper went on the auction block; Lou was the only bidder. He decided to resuscitate the *Chronicle* and his life along with it.

Which is why, on most days, I was glad my new boss hadn't kicked the bucket. The guy was bringing respect back. Too bad he was driving me and the rest of the staff nuts doing it.

I SLIPPED INTO the office at half past four that afternoon, dead time for a morning paper.

"Sorry I dumped the photos and ran this morning," I told Lou. He reminded me of a scowling basset hound hunched over my desk, pounding the keyboard with his big paws. His perpetually bloodshot eyes squinted at the computer.

"I'll give you a break this time," Kendricks replied. "But only because you got the picture to us before deadline. By the way, Chief Weathers was furious about that."

Kendricks slapped a few more keys, then rolled his chair away so I could sit.

"The chief called?"

"Yeah. Told me you weren't coming in because he'd ordered you to take care of your mother. He flipped when I told him about the photo and then pumped him for the story."

"I'd have given you more this morning, but I couldn't worm it out of him."

Lou shrugged. I relaxed and sat on the edge of my desk, happy I hadn't received a Kendricks tongue-lashing.

"So how's your mom?" he asked. "Did she actually see the woman jump?"

"Jump?"

"Yeah. The chief said she took a flying leap; your mom tried to stop her."

"It would have been nice if one of them had let me know. Mom's okay. She told me to quit hovering, so I thought I'd come in and finish the Rudy Clark story." I nodded at my computer. "You're taking a look at it?"

"After he blustered in here this morning, followed fifteen minutes later by his campaign treasurer, Ken Romano, who was balancing on a set of wobbly crutches and protesting his son's innocence, I figured I'd better read what you have. It might be a passable piece—if you get Clark's side and clean up the grammar."

"Clark's been dodging me. I applied some pressure this morning, but things didn't go as planned."

"I heard. You owe him another chance. Call him, polish it up, maybe we'll use it on page one tomorrow. Right now all I have is a rehash of the teacher negotiations that your coworker's struggling over. What else do you have?"

"Marijuana," I said.

Lou gave an exaggerated sigh. "I can see I'll have to make up some kind of employee drug policy now."

"Police busted another kid for possession last night. I think this is bigger than a few teens experimenting with weed and want to dig into it some more."

"Good idea. Did you get that off the dispatch log?"

"Yep."

"So it'll be on TV and we didn't have it today," Lou said in a way that made me feel about twelve inches tall. "Should I tune in to learn what else we're missing?"

"There was one other incident, a trespasser at the Elk Ridge Hunt and Fish Club. Not much to it."

"Someone else trying to catch a glimpse of Lord Grey's palace? From what I hear, no one gets inside the club's fence."

"Not unless they're invited. Security is unbelievable. Gord told me it was a drunk and she puked all over the back seat of the new detective's sedan when he gave her a ride back to town."

"Doesn't sound like anything we can use. What else you have going this week?"

"I thought I'd follow up on the dead woman."

"Not much meat on that bone, either. Do a brief when they release the name."

"A brief?"

Gina Holt interrupted, yelling across the room, "I've a camper on a cell phone who says a cop car just came squealing into Tourist Park with lights flashing and sirens wailing."

"I'm on it," I said, grabbing a notebook.

FIVE

ONCE AT THE PARK ENTRANCE, I couldn't miss the action. A patrol car with light bar flashing and Gordon's unmarked white sedan were parked in front of the first campsite. They were about fifty yards inside the wooden totem-pole entrance gate. Beyond the vehicles, my new buddy, Detective Freeman, was wasting several rolls of yellow tape to barricade the site. It looked more like a construction zone than a crime scene.

I parked in the visitor space at the nearby campground office, snapped a few photos through the telephoto lens and strolled across the road to Greenleaf's sedan. Gord was talking on his cell phone and jotting notes in a pad on the car's roof.

Cowboy Cop saw me approaching.

"Hey, newsman!" he yelled. "Fair warning: You cross the line this time and your next ride will be in the back of my car. The chief's not here to rescue you this go around, pal."

I lifted my camera and snapped a few photos of him pointing a finger at me. I caught the red flashing light reflecting from a Dot's Pots latrine in the background.

"Nice wheels," I said. "But don't detectives get unmarked cars?"

He glared and mumbled something about making me pay for that remark.

On the far side, campers lounged in canvas chairs, watching the scene and popping open cans of beer and soda. There were few trees to block their view and no brush or undergrowth to speak of, most of it having been trampled over years of use.

"They found her car over at Eagle's Cliff," Greenleaf said as he snapped his phone shut. I turned to see him shielding his eyes from the flashing light. "I'll handle things here, Archie. Why don't you head over to the park and keep an eye on the car until the chief gets there. And, uh…better keep the lights off and save the yellow tape. The chief said to keep it low-key."

Freeman gave me another dirty look, grabbed a sheet of paper Greenleaf handed him and stepped over to the patrol car.

"Looks like you're tonight's entertainment, Gord," I said, nodding at the growing crowd of spectators.

The Cowboy flipped on his siren and spun his wheels out of the park. Greenleaf watched him, shaking his head.

"He's from Flint," Gord said, as if this explained everything about the overzealous detective. "He'll lighten up once he settles in and gets to know the town."

"Sure," I said, thinking I'd better watch my back. There are a lot of remote roads surrounding Apostle Bay and I was sure to meet him on one before long. "So, who's the dead woman? Mom's not talking, but I'm guessing it's someone she knew or recognized."

"I doubt that. She's not a local." Greenleaf nodded toward the tent and gear on the campsite's picnic table. "She lived here the last few days."

"How'd you find her car? Campground registration?"

"Get this. It's a Caddy, older model but seems a bit high-class considering this camp. We didn't connect it to the suicide this morning because it's registered to some guy."

"You got a name?"

Greenleaf smiled and shook his head. "Not until the chief says okay."

"Did the fall kill her, or did she drown?"

"Your mom is the only one who knows for sure—until the ME finishes. She had a nasty wound on the back of her head—probably hit the rocks on the way down. I'll need to talk to your mom tonight or tomorrow. The chief kept her under wraps this morning because she was so upset."

"Give her a call. In fact, let me know what she says. She's not talking to me. She's at home now, watching Glory. I'm heading over there soon."

Gord's cell phone rang. "Excuse me."

He unclipped the phone from his belt and stepped away. I watched him lean on his car's roof to write something, hesitated, then ducked under a gap in the police tape. A faded maroon dome tent fluttered with the occasional breeze. A cast-iron fry pan and a foam cooler lay on the weathered picnic table. Crushed Budweiser cans overflowed the fire ring. It was not at all like the nearby campsites with outdoor furniture, woodpiles and multicolored towels hanging to dry on jerry-rigged clotheslines.

I glanced toward Greenleaf, saw the detective still talking and writing. The spectators seemed bored and not paying attention. I slid my pen into the cooler's cover and lifted. About three inches of dirty water filled the bottom.

I moved toward the tent, checked Greenleaf again, then stooped and peered inside. A pea-green sleeping bag lay crumpled on the tent floor. Next to it was a day pack with clothes spilling out, a small black plastic flashlight and a composition notebook. I unzipped the tent, careful to keep the sound down, reached through the open door, turned the notebook toward me and flipped it open. Sharp cursive writing filled the pages. Entries were dated, like a diary. I checked again to make sure Greenleaf wasn't watching, then turned the pages, hoping to spy a name.

Elk Ridge caught my eye. The club's name was on several pages, along with Vanessa Grey, matron of the club. Her name was circled in red. I flipped a few more pages until the writing ended. Halfway down the last page, I saw another name and address, circled with red. The writer had scratched sharp, double lines under the name, scoring through the page.

"What are you doing?"

I jerked back, flipping the book closed, and bumped into Greenleaf.

"Sorry, Gord."

"You can't mess with this stuff. The chief would

have my head if he knew you were here. Go. Get outside the tape."

I looked back toward the journal, then stood and walked to the perimeter.

"Sorry, Gord."

"You're way out of line, Vince," he said, shaking his head. "Sometimes you push it too far."

"You're right," I mumbled, but I wasn't listening. Instead, I was wondering why my mother's name and phone number were the last things the dead woman had written.

Greenleaf grabbed my arm.

"Are you paying attention? This is serious. You could really burn me with a stunt like that."

"I wouldn't do that." I forced a smile. "If I wasn't welcome in your office, where else could I get my morning caffeine fix?"

"I think you should— What are you looking at?"

I stared past Greenleaf at a white camper heading toward us. A red dancer graced the side.

"I saw that camper at Eagle's Cliff this morning when I was taking Mom home. You think they were around when the woman jumped?"

"Let's find out," Greenleaf said.

SIX

TOM AND MAISY REYNOLDS loved square dancing and bird watching. They told us that they traveled the country in their camper, June to September, searching for dances and new birds to add to their life lists. Their course followed migration patterns and a dance schedule discovered on the Internet.

Tom said in his slow, elongated drawl, "It's a great way to see the country and stay in shape."

Tom and Maisy, both wearing scarlet Western shirts with fringe across the chest, had climbed from the truck when Gord waved them over.

"What can we do for you folks?" Tom asked. He put his elbows on the truck's hood as if leaning on a split-rail fence to shoot the breeze with neighbors. He moved languidly and I suspected he did everything, maybe even square dance, in slow motion. Thick brown hair showed under his Stetson when he raised the brim.

Greenleaf flashed his badge and introduced himself.

"Is this about what happened this morning?" Tom asked. "We talked to the police chief about it. He's a nice guy, the chief. Are you from the same department?"

I noticed Greenleaf stiffen, but he kept smiling and leaned on the truck's hood also. Maisy joined them, everybody leaning on the truck except me. Maisy's shoulders barely cleared the hood. Her khaki-blond hair hung down to the center of her back in a single braid.

"Chief Weathers?" Greenleaf asked. "A big guy, crew cut, silver hair?"

"That's him."

"He's my boss. Where did he catch up with you?"

"In our camper," Maisy said. "We were sipping coffee after all the commotion. Earlier, when that woman jumped, Tom and I had been glassing gulls. I spotted a Bonaparte's gull there last night, and we wanted to see if it was still around."

Greenleaf nodded. "They show up here from time to time."

What a scammer, I thought. We'd been friends since high school, since Greenleaf quarterbacked the football team through a dismal season, while I rode the bench with a broken leg. I'd cracked my femur while racing to, and stumbling over, the water cooler during practice— hardly the illustrious career Doc Marshall envisioned when he named me after the great coach Lombardi. Anyway, in all that time, Gord never mentioned an interest in ornithology, especially gull species.

"Did you see it again this morning?" Greenleaf asked.

"Nah, only ring-billed and glaucous gulls," Tom said.

"But you saw her jump?"

"No," Tom said. "Like we told the chief, we weren't that close. All we heard was the argument and then something that could have been a splash."

"The argument?" I asked.

"Sure," Maisy said, turning to me. "Well, we couldn't really hear the argument. I mean, we couldn't hear what they were saying. We just heard two women's voices. Sounded like they were yelling. The chief told us that one woman was trying to talk the other out of jumping."

"She didn't convince her, I guess," Tom said.

"Maybe that's why she was yelling so loudly," Maisy said. "She sounded…mad. They both did."

"You didn't see her jump?" Greenleaf asked again.

"No," the couple said in unison.

"Did you see who was arguing? How do you know it was two women?"

"We didn't see them," Tom said.

"But we heard women's voices," Maisy added. "I'm pretty sure of that."

"Did you hear anything they said?" I asked.

Tom and Maisy both shook their heads. "Sorry," they said, again in unison.

"When did Chief Weathers interview you?" Greenleaf asked.

"After everyone cleared out," Tom said. "He came knocking on the camper's door. Say, you don't want us to hang around, do you? The chief said it was okay for us to leave. We're heading to Wisconsin first thing in the a.m. There's a dance tomorrow night."

"An excellent caller," Maisy said. "We'd sure hate to miss it."

"I'm not asking you to stay," Greenleaf said. "I'm really sorry to have stopped you. It's been a busy day and the chief and I haven't had a chance to compare notes.

Did he get your names and address in case we have any other questions?"

"We gave him our card," Maisy said.

"The best way to get in touch with us when we're on the road is the cell," Tom said. "Sometimes we can check our e-mail too."

Tom pulled a stack of business cards out of his wallet and handed one to Greenleaf.

"I'll take one, too," I said.

Greenleaf shot me a glare as Tom leaned over and passed a card to Maisy, who handed it to me.

"Sorry again to have held you up," Greenleaf said. "Thanks for your time."

We all shook hands before the couple climbed back into their truck and drove away. Their camper was through the entrance when a black Crown Victoria sped into the park, trailing a cloud of dust behind it.

"All hail to the chief," I said. "He didn't tell you about those folks, did he?"

SEVEN

THE CHIEF SLID IN next to Gordon's sedan. Dust and his harsh baritone growl overtook us a second later. Godfather was yelling through his open window as he unbuckled.

"What the heck are you doing here, Vince? You're supposed to be at your mother's house. And why didn't you take her straight home as I told you?"

"You know Mom as well as I do, Chief. She doesn't want me around and it's pointless to argue when her mind's made up. Although, it might have helped if you had clued me in on the argument she had with the victim."

"Wha— Who told you that?"

"Tom and Maisy Reynolds."

I could see the chief winding up to yell again. Greenleaf interrupted.

"They just stopped on their way out of the campground," Greenleaf said. "They mentioned you'd interviewed them."

"Motormouth tourists talk too much," Weathers said. "I didn't say anything because your mother needs a son now, not a reporter trying to interview her. If she wants to tell you, she will. Don't pester her about it."

"But—"

Weathers interrupted, "Look, I know you're curious, Vince. I know you're thinking like a reporter, too—that you can't help doing that. But this is a suicide, nothing else. I already called Kendricks and gave him the story. I told him to lay off because of your mom. So you back off, too. And don't pull another stunt like bringing a camera across the police line when you have family to worry about."

He turned to Greenleaf. "Did you send Archie over to watch the car?"

"He should be there now," Greenleaf said.

"I'll wrap things up here myself, then go check it out. You head back to the office, Gord. And, Vince, go home."

I saw Greenleaf raise an eyebrow in surprise. Strange for the chief to dismiss him and take on the grunt work.

"You're right, Chief," I said. "See you in the morning."

I started walking, then jogged toward my Bronco. Maybe, I thought, I could get a look at the woman's car before Weathers got there.

EIGHT

I DROVE THE TEN-MINUTE TRIP to Eagle's Cliff glancing more at the rearview mirror and my handheld police scanner than at the road. The scanner stayed silent—no surprise considering the local cops use their cell phones more than radios these days.

The single-lane park road followed the peninsula's outline. Every half-mile, scenic turnouts widened the road and a few cars could stop without impeding the one-way traffic. At the peninsula's point, the road spilled into a parking lot.

During summer a steady stream of tourists and locals cruised the road—the tourists sightseeing and looking for deer, the locals checking out the tourists. During the fall-color season, cars jammed the pavement, and the ten-minute circuit around the peninsula took about thirty.

I came up behind three cars creeping along. The driver of the middle car dangled a carrot out of the window, as if baiting animals to follow. The lead car stopped when it crested a hill. The driver's door swung open and a man carrying a camera stepped out. I saw a doe and a yearling step onto the road. Two kids, elementary-school age, stepped from the second car. They carried apples toward the deer.

I drummed my hands on the wheel, checked my mirror again, then pulled left to the road's edge, inching past the logjam, brushing tree branches with my Bronco. The third car in the line pulled behind me. The deer stared at me, then sauntered out of my way while deer feeders shot me dirty looks. I ought to sic Freeman on them, I thought, since feeding deer is illegal in the park. Heck, he'd probably have them all—kids, too—in handcuffs by the time he was done.

As I pulled away, I saw the car behind me stop and I smiled. The driver and passenger climbed out, blocking the road.

At the gravel lot, I pulled in behind Freeman's patrol car. This time he had the lights off. He stepped from his vehicle and signaled me to move on, but I acted as if I didn't understand and killed the engine. Then I stepped from the car and walked straight at him.

"A Cadillac Seville?" I asked. I pointed at a dust-covered gold car. "Not what I would have guessed considering the campsite."

"Don't you know how to mind you own business?" Freeman asked.

"Why don't we start over, Detective?" I said, holding my hands up as a gesture of submission. "We're going to see a lot of each other, so we might as well get along."

I moved to step around him and catch a better look at the car. Freeman sidestepped to block me.

"Don't even think about it," he said. "Run along back to whatever hole you crawled out of."

"How about we meet for coffee tomorrow after my deadline? Have a little get-to-know-you chat. Coffee's on me."

"Is that a bribe? 'Cause it sounds like one to me." On the car's trunk I saw a bumper sticker: THIS CAR PROTECTED BY SMITH AND WESSON. The tags were special Native American plates from the Rum River reservation in Wisconsin. A sticker on the upper-right corner of the rear window said EMPLOYEE PARKING—RUM RIVER CASINO.

"C'mon, Detective," I said. "Loosen up. A cup of coffee to welcome you to town. No strings."

He stepped into my personal space, leaned his face a few inches from my nose and growled, "Get lost."

"It's an open invitation if you change your mind."

I climbed back in the Bronco, leaned out the window to snap a few photos of the car until Freeman blocked the view, then pulled onto the road. Through the woods I heard a siren kick on and I knew the chief was here. I silently thanked the tourists.

NINE

GLORY DID HER BEST to saturate me and our cramped bathroom during her bubble bath that night. In vain I struggled to keep some part of myself dry and get some part of her clean. What a battle.

Fifteen minutes into it, Glory screeched and pressed a foam-covered fist against her eye.

"C'mon, baby, it's the soap," I said. "Let me wipe it."

I grabbed a towel, tried to wipe her face, but she struggled and screamed more.

The portable phone rang.

I pulled her from the water and wrapped her in a towel. My voice kicked on in the bedroom—the answering-machine greeting.

"C'mon, let me wipe this."

Glory grabbed a slack piece of towel and rubbed her face. She stopped crying. I sat on the toilet, pulling her into my lap, then grabbed the portable phone off the vanity, where it rested by my cell phone.

"Hello," I said, interrupting the message.

There was a long pause, then, "Let me speak with Deb please."

"She's out," I said. "Who's calling?"

"Ken Romano, from the school board."

Ken Romano, who also owned the local car dealership, was Clark's campaign treasurer and father of the boy who got a break. I'm sure I wasn't his favorite person at the moment.

"Is this Vince?"

"Yeah, Ken. This isn't a good time. My hands are full."

Glory squirmed. I lowered her to the floor.

"Sure. I'll catch Deb tomorrow," Romano said. "I'm surprised she's not home."

"Is your meeting over?"

Glory scooted toward the tub and pulled herself up against the side.

"We finished at least an hour ago."

"No, honey, bath is over."

"What?"

"Sorry. My daughter is trying to take a swim. Did you say the meeting's been over awhile?"

"Yeah. The teachers left some time ago. The board met alone afterward. That's what I was calling about." He paused, then lowered his voice as if someone could overhear us. "You've got a smart wife there, Vince. She's a tough cookie, but I can tell she's fair. Too bad the other teachers on the bargaining committee are steering her down the wrong road. Especially Tony Wittmer. It's been getting kind of ugly. But I shouldn't talk about this with you."

"You're right," I said. Deb and I had an agreement not to talk about the teachers' contract negotiations. I didn't want to get blamed if something showed up in the paper or have her take the heat for it from her coworkers. Our other reporter, Mort Maki, was covering the story.

"There's no message. I'll call Deb tomorrow. Uh…by the way, are you still going to run that story—"

My cell phone chirped, and at the same time Glory swung her leg over the tub. I dropped the portable phone as she fell sideways, splashing into the water.

I lifted her clear and hugged her against my chest while she coughed.

"That's what you get for climbing back into the tub, kiddo."

Glory chose that moment to relieve herself.

AN HOUR LATER we were both dry and Glory was protesting bedtime from her crib with yet another crying jag. I remembered the cell call, checked my phone and recognized Gord's home number on the caller ID. I dialed.

"Hey, Gord, it's Vince. You called?"

"Man, you could have cost me my job today."

"I said I'm sorry. Besides, there was no harm done."

"I'm not talking about the tent incident, which, now that you remind me, was a stupid stunt, too. I'm talking about after that. When Freeman told Weathers you'd been to the car, he blew a gasket."

"Why? The car was on public property and guarded by that Clint Eastwood wannabe. What did he think I was going to do? Steal it? Corrupt evidence? It's a suicide. Don't you think he's overreacting a little?"

Greenleaf was silent.

"What did you learn at the campsite?"

"You're getting nada from me, including the woman's name. The chief's orders. He actually said this case is going to die a quiet death, just like that woman."

"Case?"

Greenleaf was silent again. Glory's cries grew louder, and I put a finger over my free ear.

"Is Glory okay?" Greenleaf asked.

"She doesn't want to be in bed."

"Shouldn't you go get her or something?"

I walked further from Glory's room.

"You have to let her cry it out, Gord. See what fatherhood is all about? Now, what aren't you telling me? I can hear it in your voice. There's more to this."

"What did you see in that journal?" Greenleaf asked.

"What journal?"

"Give me a break. What did you see?"

"Why are you asking me?"

"Weathers took the journal and everything else at the campsite after he sent me away. He made it clear he didn't want me going through the stuff. Now I'm curious."

"Tell me her name."

"No way."

I hesitated a moment, then told Greenleaf about Elk Ridge and Vanessa Grey being in the journal. I excluded the info about Mom. Greenleaf didn't seem surprised, and something clicked.

"That trespasser Freeman picked up at the club and brought back to Tourist Park, the one who doused his car in vomit—she's the dead woman, isn't she?"

No response.

"C'mon, Gordo. I'm right, aren't I?"

"That's all you saw in the journal?" Greenleaf asked. "No other names or information that might explain why she was here?"

"It's not as if I had much time to read it before you interrupted."

"Sure," he said. "Maybe the chief's worried about keeping Elk Ridge out of this. They're kind of touchy about publicity. That's got to be it."

"You don't sound overly convinced."

"You're right about the trespasser."

"What's her name?"

"You want that, you've got to do the homework."

TEN

THE SLAMMING CAR DOOR woke me. I pulled my face out of the couch cushion and glanced at Glory sleeping in the chair across from me, then listened to Deb enter through the rear door. Closet hangers jangled, her keys hit the counter, the floor by the sink squeaked. Then I heard water running.

"Oh, you're still awake," Deb said a moment later. "Sorry it's so late." Then she saw Glory. "You couldn't get her in bed again?" Did I hear a hint of "Just what I expected" in her voice?

"She'd have nothing to do with the crib," I said. "Screamed like a banshee. I tried your various suggestions to calm her, and I tried to wait her out, but I couldn't take it after a while. She just won't go to bed for me."

Deb kneeled by the chair and caressed Glory's hair.

"She'll come around. Give her time. By the way, how's your mom?"

"Fine. I called tonight. She told me to quit bothering her, and Glory was crying in the background, so that didn't help." I hadn't asked Mom why her name was in the journal. I'd do that face to face tomorrow.

"That must be a freaky thing, finding a body. Do you know who she was yet?"

"Someone from Wisconsin. The chief said she jumped and Mom tried to stop her."

"Maybe that explains why your mom's upset."

"Maybe. By the way, Ken Romano called."

Deb stopped caressing Glory and looked up.

"As a matter of fact, he called about two hours ago."

"He's not supposed to do that."

"What? He's not supposed to call? Where were you?"

"We were going over the school board's latest proposal—"

"We?"

"The bargaining committee," Deb said. "We've been sitting in the corner booth at Hardees. You want to call the manager and check?"

"It took a couple of hours to go over their proposal?"

"Why are you angry? You're the one who suggested I join the committee. You said I should get involved with the teachers again before school started. As I recall, you said this would be a good experience for me."

"I know, but I didn't realize it meant so many late nights for you."

"School starts in two weeks, Vince. We go back to the classroom in one. We need a contract. And when else can we meet? I take care of Glory during the day. The school board members all have jobs. You've covered education before. Get with it. All the meetings are at night or on weekends."

"All of them? What about your daytime meetings with

Wittmer?" Glory stirred and I realized I was getting too loud. "By the way," I whispered, "Romano didn't have anything nice to say about him."

"Romano has no business talking to you about teachers or contract stuff."

I saw Glory's eyes open. She looked up at her mother and then yawned.

"Hi, little Morning Glory," Deb said. "Let's get you into bed." She scooped Glory into her arms and carried her across the room. At the doorway to Glory's room, she turned back toward me. "I asked Tony about the other students." I gave her a blank look so she added, "You know, the other kids arrested this summer. Considering your animosity toward him, however, I'm not sure I should tell you what he thinks."

"Oh, he has a theory?"

"He's sure they were all set up. And he thinks he knows who's doing it."

"Yeah, right."

Deb turned and carried Glory to bed.

ELEVEN

If Lou Kendricks had a bed at the *Chronicle*'s office, I couldn't find it—and I'd searched. No matter how early I arrived, or how late I left the newsroom, I found Lou there. Lack of sleep probably accounted for his blood-shot eyes—that and the stink of solvents and ink down in the press room, where he spent more time than most editorial employees.

I grabbed the coffeepot, noticed a telltale Kendricks-chewed pencil stub by the sugar canister and inhaled the aroma of a fresh brew. I carried the pot to Lou's work-station and studied the four half-full stained mugs on the desk.

"I know the two with mold growing in them aren't today's cups, Lou. Should I pour this into one of the others?"

Lou grunted, moved his mouse to copy a wire story, then reached into a drawer and pulled out a new cup, which he slapped on the desk with enough force I expected it to shatter.

"This industry is going down the tubes," he said. "Half these stories look as if a child wrote them. Who hires these people? Who edits this junk? And what is all this nonsense about unnamed sources?"

This was the daily Kendricks diatribe—Lou spouted some version of it on most days: Young reporters have no ethics; they learned reporting from reality TV; newspapers were once a ten-course meal, and now they're junk food.

He sounded like a dinosaur, but I had to admit he was right about some things. And the *Chronicle* was a far better paper since Lou bought it. I was a better reporter.

"You're here early," he said. He grabbed the wrong mug, sipped and acted as if he didn't notice the coffee was cold and growing hair.

"I'd like to say it was to make up for running out yesterday. But that's not why."

"Is your mom hanging in?"

"She's fine. I'd like to slip away after deadline to check on her."

"If you must. Make up the time later. Did you get in touch with the prosecutor?"

"Yesterday evening. I had to listen to his usual load of manure, but he made a statement. It's in the story. Something about Ken Junior being a good citizen who led police to the other offenders. Police were mistaken about the circumstances in his arrest, he said. The statement implies Ken Junior was a hero. I called the parents of the other kids. They didn't think he was so heroic. Those comments are in the story, too."

"Good. Is your idea about the local drug epidemic going anywhere?"

"Not yet." I made a mental note to ask Deb about Tony's theory after things cooled between us.

"Anything else for today?"

"I can put something together on the Eagle's Cliff jumper. She was camping at Tourist Park. That's why the cops were there yesterday."

"They give you a name?"

"The cops aren't saying a thing. That's why I'm here early. Greenleaf stood me up this morning, and the chief was in a meeting."

"Doesn't sound as if you have much," Kendricks said. "Is Dale Weathers changing his mind about suicide?"

"Not that I'm aware."

"Then give me a news brief when they release the name."

"I know the name. April Coyote, fifty-two, of the Rum River reservation in Wisconsin."

"How did you get a name if no one's talking? And don't say an unnamed source."

"Remember I mentioned that disturbance at Elk Ridge? The trespasser? Her name was April Coyote. I looked up the report this morning. They owned the same car, had the same address. They're the same person."

"Did the cops confirm it?"

"Um, not officially."

"Then you've done good work, but it was a waste of time because we won't use it. Not unless you're saying the club security guards drove her crazy and caused her to jump. Scare up something else for this morning."

Wow, I thought on my way back to the coffee table. I'd hoped for a bit more enthusiasm or maybe a pat on the back. Instead I'd be scrambling for another story this morning.

I slid into my desk and started flipping through the Rolodex for ideas, but couldn't get April Coyote off my mind. Maybe, I wondered, it was time for me to explore a feature on Native American casinos.

TWELVE

MORT MAKI'S METABOLISM must run in hyperdrive. This guy inhales food but is skeleton thin. I see him chowing breakfast every morning at the Laughing Whitefish while I'm heading to the cop shop. Then, when he gets into the office, he drops his battered canvas briefcase on the desk and heads to our employee lounge, where he shovels in a brown-bag lunch—usually two baloney and Velveeta on white bread sandwiches, a bag of chips and a Shasta orange soda. After that he bums food from the staff for the rest of the day, or when he strikes out on that, he empties the vending machine. Gina quit filling her candy jar because Mort ate it all. Others hide their lunches and discreetly snatch bites when they think Mort's not looking.

He chomps while talking, crunches while typing and consumes upward of half a gallon of sugar-and-cream-laced coffee each day. He looks like a pasty distance runner addicted to diet pills.

Personally, I don't mind the guy. We go our own way, do our own things and rarely squabble over stories. He'd rather stay by his desk and work the phones; I'd rather be out. It makes for an easy way to split the work. I doubt he'd ever pass things my way, but I wouldn't do the same for him, so I guess that's fair.

After my short chat with Lou, I worked the phones awhile but not too many people were in so I scanned the wire for interesting stuff and entered a few briefs while I waited for Mort to arrive. When he made for the lounge, I grabbed my mug and followed.

The lounge is a windowless room with a scratched conference table, four hard-plastic chairs that wobble, a waist-high refrigerator that gives new meaning to the word disgusting and two vending machines. It's a great place for a private conversation because most employees avoid the dingy room and eat at their desks, or, during the few months when the weather is agreeable, they eat outside.

"Hi Mort." I sat opposite him.

"Thanks for sticking me with that Eagle's Cliff suicide," Maki said. Gobs of white bread and processed cheese stuck to his teeth. "Kendricks gave me ten seconds to put something together, and then he ranted when I couldn't. You could have at least given me some notes when you sent the camera in."

"I'm sorry about that. Thanks for covering it. You probably heard my mom discovered the body, and she was a bit broken up. I was taking care of her, and that's why I didn't finish it."

"You had time to take the photo. Get the good credit first, and then take care of your mom. That's vintage Marshall. Can't believe Lou let you off the hook so easy."

Maki shoved the last of his sandwich into his mouth and opened his chip bag.

"C'mon, Mort, I took the photo before I found my mom. Anyway, I'm sorry. Let me offer you something. You probably already know, but in case you hadn't heard, the school board and teachers met again last night. School starts in two weeks, and they still aren't close to an agreement."

"I know school starts in two weeks. Tell me something I don't know."

That meant he didn't know they'd met last night, I thought. "It's the best I can do for you."

"Are you deciding to help me now?" Maki asked. Chip crumbs fell onto his shirt. He picked them off and popped them into his mouth. "'Cause if you are, tell your wife to talk to me. I'm getting squat from the teachers' union."

"Look, you can call her, but I don't know what she'll say. I don't even know what the issues are. I only know about the meetings because I have daddy duty while Deb's out. Actually, I'm kind of curious how it's going. What do you think of the teachers' bargaining team?"

"You spying on Deb?" Maki lifted an eyebrow in surprise.

"Nah. Just curious about who's working with her. How about that guy Tony?"

"Wittmer?"

"Yeah." I grimaced inside about how transparent this must sound. "What's he like?"

"He's God's gift to the teaching world. Didn't you

know that? He's a true believer in making sure the students' interests come first. It's all hooey, of course. But he's convincing, and that's why the school board hates him."

"How do you know he's full of it?"

"My neighbor's kid had him as a teacher last year. Her son said he always chummed up to the girls. He does have a reputation with the ladies, I hear."

"From who?"

"It's just the word around town. Better watch out with him near Deb." Maki sneered and winked. "Though she might not be young enough."

"Thanks." I dumped the last of my coffee—cold now—down my throat and walked back to the newsroom.

THIRTEEN

WHEN THE *CHRONICLE*'s printing press cranks up each morning, it shakes the entire building. Desks vibrate, coffee splashes out of full mugs, pencils roll astray.

Lou shudders along with the ancient rollers. It's like a symbiotic trembling, as if he's using his own will to help the beast overcome inertia and spin paper again.

After the rumbling reaches a crescendo and the drums smooth to a hypnotic thunking, you can see Kendricks mouth a brief prayer of thanks.

I waited through the morning ritual, then knowing the paper was in bed walked out of the *Chronicle,* crossed the street and bought two blueberry muffins. I'd called Mom earlier in the morning, during her regular power-walk time so she couldn't argue, and left a message on her machine: "I'll bring a little snack around 11:00 a.m." I was surprised she hadn't called back to dissuade me and half expected to find her house empty. Instead I found the chief's car in her driveway.

Called in reinforcements, I thought.

Inside I found Weathers and Mom at the kitchen table. The chief's dress uniform looked as stiff as cardboard. Mom was dressed for yard work.

"Did I interrupt something?" I asked.

"Not at all," Mom said, rising from her kitchen table and taking plates to the sink. "Dale stopped by to check on me. I should be flattered—all you guys visiting."

"Sorry about the muffins," I said, dropping the bag on the table. "I'd have picked up an extra if I knew you had company."

Weathers pushed himself away from the table. "Not to worry. I have to get back to work. Loretta, how about I pick up something from the Laughing Whitefish for dinner and stop by after work?"

"Thanks, Dale, but I'm fine. Really." She placed a hand on his arm. "Thanks for stopping by."

"Vince, walk me out to my car," Weathers ordered.

Here comes another lecture.

Weathers waited until we were outside with the door closed before looking at me. I decided to go on the offensive.

"I know the dead woman is April Coyote."

"We don't have a positive ID yet"—Weathers held up his hand before I could interrupt—"but you're probably right. After we can locate the next of kin, you'll get a news release, as you always do. It may take a few days."

"A few days? C'mon."

"It's not as easy as you think. There are…complications."

"Like what?"

"It's a suicide and it's not even someone from this area. Drop it." Weathers put his hand on my shoulder. "Vince, I'm worried about Loretta. You've got to leave her alone on this."

He gave me an awkward pat, then walked to his car. He looked back before climbing in. "Don't try to make this into something for your own personal gain, Vince. You'll only hurt the people you love."

FOURTEEN

"I SUPPOSE YOU WANT to talk about yesterday," Mom said. She stood ten feet inside the door, ready for battle, her arms crossed and eyes narrow. "Isn't that why you're here?"

"The chief just warned me to leave you alone."

"I told him that would just goad you into asking more. But he's used to giving orders, not taking them."

"Truth is, Mom, I'm starting to wonder why he's trying so hard to keep me out of this. And his own detectives, too. It seems a little odd."

"It's because you can be a pain in the rear, Vince. Anyway, I'd rather talk about you and Deb. I want to know what's going on between you two."

"What?"

"You think I'm blind and deaf? You've been grouchy. You both seem to walk on eggshells when I'm around. What's the story?"

This was just like her, change the subject, going on the attack. "The story, Mom, is who died at Eagle's Cliff yesterday? That's the story."

"No, it's not. That was nothing."

"Really?" I said, voice rising. "Then tell me why your name was in April Coyote's journal. Circled in red. It was the last thing she wrote before dying, Mom. She came looking for you yesterday."

Mom held my eyes for a moment, then the fire went out, her chin dropped to her chest and she sagged against the wall.

"Did Dale tell you that?"

"No. Like I just said, he warned me off. He's even hiding it from his staff. He doesn't know I saw the journal."

"Let's sit down," she said. She turned and walked toward the kitchen, looking older than I remembered. I caught up and put my arm around her as we passed through the door.

"I'll tell you what I know. And when I finish, you're going to talk about what's going on with you and Deb." But there was no conviction in her voice now.

Mom's kitchen faced south. Sun streamed through a French door, bathing her garden of houseplants. The room's cheer seemed absurd at this moment. We sat in opposite chairs, ignoring the muffins.

"That woman followed me out to the rocks. She really wanted your father. Since he's dead, she came for me."

"Why?"

"She accused Doc of causing her sister's death."

"Why would she think that?"

"He used to hear that occasionally. When a patient died, their family blamed him. Sometimes he used to believe it. Your father always took his cases too personally."

"But that must have been years ago. Why was she here now?"

"People need someone to blame. From what I gather, she only learned about her sister's death last month even though it happened years ago."

"Did she"—I recalled the broken easel—"attack you?"

"No."

"Why didn't you tell me this yesterday?"

"Because I wanted to protect you."

"From what?"

"From things you don't need to hear."

I leaned back, wondering why she thought this would bother me.

"She'd written Elk Ridge Hunt and Fish Club in her journal, too," I said. "And Vanessa Grey. I wonder what her beef was with them."

Mom tried to hide it, but I saw her eyes flare briefly at the mention of Vanessa Grey. Instead of answering, she just shrugged her shoulders.

FIFTEEN

BACK AT THE NEWSPAPER, I dug through my Rolodex until I found the Elk Ridge number. It was a prize I'd found while going through my father's desk some years back. The members paid good money to keep outsiders off club property, but before the place had its own on-site medical staff, Doc Marshall had been called to deal with emergencies.

"Hello."

They'd have caller ID and know it was the *Chronicle* calling.

"I'd like to make an appointment with Vanessa Grey please."

The person snorted. "Who's this?"

"Vince Marshall from the *Apostle Chronicle*. We're doing a feature on her family's history and their importance to the region. Grey Industries is the largest employer in Northern Michigan."

"How did you get this number?"

"In fact, the Grey family has been vital to not only the regional economy, but also the national economy. They are the leader in steel production. Do you think I can see her this afternoon or maybe first thing tomorrow? We'd like to use the piece for the Sunday edition."

"Bud, she's not going to see you tonight, tomorrow or ever. Try the public-relations department."

"Well, I tried that—"

I heard the dial tone. I hung up and decided to try something else. A year earlier I'd written a story about the club trying to qualify its land as a historic landmark. The move would have exempted it from real-estate taxes. Man, there was a story that angered the locals. Almost a third of our county's annual revenue comes from the club, and Elk Ridge's owners can afford to pay what is surely a small sum to them.

The Associated Press picked up the story and the case made national news for a day. The club later dropped its plan when a judge ruled the public had the right to visit any land in the historic register.

Harlan Amos Montgomery III had been the club's lawyer and spokesman at the time. I figured he was my best option. Lawyers like to talk, billable hours and all. I found his number and dialed. He was, of course, out of the office.

"Could you please contact him and let him know I've called about the Elk Ridge Hunt and Fish Club. I'm working on a story about a suspicious death. The police are investigating his client's involvement."

Montgomery returned my call forty minutes later. "Mr. Marshall? You're the same reporter I talked to about a year ago?"

"Yes, sir."

"You didn't make any friends at Elk Ridge."

"It would have been hard to put a good spin on the

club's plan, even if I'd wanted to. Though you gave it a valiant effort."

"You can cease the harassment of my client, or it will be necessary for me to contact the local authorities."

"Harassment?"

"A suspicious death? Or are you working on a special feature about the Grey family? What's this all about?"

"The feature was bogus. The death isn't. Police found a dead woman in Lake Superior yesterday. She had tried to see Vanessa Grey the night before her death. The circumstances are suspicious."

"They are? I'm given to understand she committed suicide in broad daylight with witnesses. You'd do better with a little honesty. What exactly do you want?"

"I want to close up the loose ends. I'd like a few minutes of Mrs. Grey's time. Any chance of that?"

"None. However, as you well know, Grey Industries has its own public-relations firm and they could write your Sunday feature."

"Thanks, but no thanks. I'd like to talk with the old lady. I would keep the conversation off the record, if that's the only way."

"On the record, off the record, it's a meeting that won't happen."

SIXTEEN

THE PHONE RANG as soon as I replaced the receiver.

"It's Gordon. I'm in the parking lot behind your building. You have a minute?"

I FOUND GORD leaning against the brick parapet near the newspaper's garbage bin, his hands shoved deep into his pockets, his coat collar turned up against the rising north wind.

"Man, you should have told me the temperature dropped," I said, rubbing my arms. "I'd have put on a coat."

Greenleaf shrugged and looked away. He seemed uncomfortable, and I didn't think it was the wind bothering him.

Beyond Greenleaf, I saw Apostle Bay's Downtown Park, a narrow grass strip that included playground equipment, a volleyball court and horseshoe pits. The park extended two city blocks on land that once held the town's passenger railway depot.

"I missed you this morning," I said.

"I know," replied Greenleaf. "I might be tied up the next few mornings."

"With what?"

"Avoiding the press. The chief doesn't want us talking."

"C'mon, are you serious?"

"Yep. Something's out of whack. He locked the suicide file in his office. When I brought him my report today, he took it and told me not to waste any more time. He said he'd close it personally."

"What's the big secret?"

"That's what I'm hoping you'll tell me. I get the feeling this is not just about keeping the bigwigs at Elk Ridge happy. It has something to do with your mother."

"Could be. He feels he owes it to my dad to watch out for her. They were as close as brothers. Maybe closer. Did you know that when the chief's number came up for the Korean War, Dad gave up his draft deferment and joined with him?"

I recalled how the chief told me this story on my father's final night. We were waiting outside his room, giving Mom her final moments alone.

"He's overly protective of her," I said. "I don't know what else to tell you."

"I think something else happened on Eagle's Cliff yesterday," Greenleaf said. "Something you all know about and aren't telling me. I don't mind keeping my trap shut, but I don't like getting cut out."

"You think I'm holding back, Gord? C'mon. I'm trying to find out what's going on, too."

"Has your mom told you anything else?"

I chuckled. "This isn't the way it's supposed to go. I pump you for information."

"The ME said Coyote died of head trauma. She was probably dead before she hit the water."

"She hit a rock on the way down. You told me that yesterday."

"There are marks on her arms. She had bruises on both arms, just below the shoulder. Someone grabbed her forcefully. One set looks like finger marks."

I stepped forward until my thighs pressed against the parapet's cold brick.

"Maybe Elk Ridge's guards roughed her up the night before. Maybe Mom grabbed her and tried to stop her from jumping."

"Maybe," Greenleaf said.

"What are you saying?"

"I don't know—yet."

"Well, I don't know any more than I knew last night, and I spent an hour with Mom this morning. And after that I tried to get an appointment to talk with someone at Elk Ridge, to see if I could learn something there, but I can't get in."

"What about the argument Tom and Maisy Reynolds heard? What's your mom say about that?"

"Pretty much what the chief said."

"What about the tent? Did you see anything else?"

I avoided my friend's eyes. "No."

Greenleaf sighed. I rubbed my arms again and then changed the subject. "Listen, there's something else I wanted to talk to you about this morning. I've been wondering about all these kids getting caught with marijuana. Deb insists the kids involved aren't the type to experiment with drugs. What do you think is going on?"

Greenleaf stared at me as if he didn't follow the conversation change. Then he narrowed his eyes. "What's going on? I'll tell you what's going on—something that stinks, that's what. And you're all part of it."

MONTGOMERY'S CALL HAD COME while I was outside with Greenleaf, so Gina took the message. He was on a flight heading toward Minneapolis. From there he'd catch a private jet to Apostle Bay. I could have ten minutes with him and the Baroness at half past five that evening.

So much for the meeting that would never happen.

SEVENTEEN

AT LEAST THE WAITING ROOM in the Elk Ridge security office was warm, because there was little else good about the place. The seats hurt my back, window shades blocked my view, and there was nothing to read, eat or drink. Obviously the members did not venture into this place.

A short, hostile guard shaped like a whisky barrel had searched me in what felt like too personal a manner. He'd confiscated my recorder, camera, and grunted something about giving them back on the way out. He let me keep my cell phone after an argument, but only with the understanding that I'd surrender it when my ride arrived.

After an hour's wait, I suspected the security force did not believe I had an appointment and probably hadn't called to let anyone know I was here.

I flipped open my cell phone and dialed Gina.

"How are you and Glory doing?"

"Everything's great," Gina said. "She's a real sweetie. I was expecting the worst considering the way you gripe and moan. Let me guess. You're running late."

"I'm running nowhere. I don't know what's up. Are you okay with Glory a little bit longer?"

"Absolutely. We're having a good time. It's been a

while since I've had a toddler around. I miss the fun stuff."

"Fun stuff, right. Thanks for watching her. I really appreciate you doing it on such short notice."

When I hung up, I noticed the guard was now standing by the exit.

"An officer will take you up to the house now," he said, holding his palm out for the phone.

I dropped it into his hand and asked, "What took so long? The lawyer's plane late?"

"Your escort's coming through the door now."

There were some ball players in high school who made me glad I was a bench-rider because I knew they'd crush me if I ever got on the field. My escort, a few pounds south of a Humvee, would have made those guys look tiny.

"Follow me," he said.

I followed him outside. He told me to sit in the back seat of a white Escalade with the Elk Ridge logo on the side. He walked around to the driver's seat. Another guard was in the front passenger slot. We drove through the wrought-iron gate.

Five minutes later we broke from the steep, tree-lined road and into the so-called hunting camp. Even by failing light I realized the place was grander than I'd imagined.

We were on a mountaintop with a near three-sixty view. In the west, a final blaze of red-orange on the horizon was all that remained of day. North and east, Lake Superior shimmered violet.

We drove through an ostentatious facsimile of a logging town. Shiny asphalt replaced what would have been rutted, muddy roads at the turn of the century. Buildings designed to look like log cabins lined both sides of the road. The timbers were massive, probably built from the few remaining virgin red and white pines that once covered Northern Michigan. The cabins appeared to be shops. A large building at the end of the street looked like a lodge or restaurant. Beyond the town, back into the forest, slate roofs poked through the canopy. I guessed from their size that the homes underneath were gargantuan.

The SUV eased through the little town and back into the trees. We entered a long, curving drive and stopped in front of a granite castle—a real castle, complete with turrets, arched windows and a drawbridge. A stream flowed under the bridge.

Another security stud stepped from the shadows and opened my door.

"This way," he said, guiding me through a massive wood-and-iron door, through a foyer with thick rugs and pearly sconces lighting stone walls, and into some sort of parlor.

Gas logs blazed in a stone fireplace. A man with white hair, tanned face and alert eyes sat in a leather armchair sipping from a china cup. A tea service rested on a low table in front of him. Behind his chair, a portrait of a robust explorer graced the wall. I guessed the man in the painting was Baron Grey, Vanessa's father.

The far end of the room was in shadow, but I thought I saw an open door there.

The man stood slowly, with effort, when I entered the room. He did not offer his hand. "I'm Harlan Montgomery. I believe you requested a meeting."

EIGHTEEN

"YES. THANKS." I couldn't think of anything else to say so I added, "How was your flight?"

"Late and uncomfortable. I don't care for flying. And in fifteen minutes I'm heading back to the airport. I intend to be home for my great-grandson's christening tomorrow. What do you want?"

Montgomery grabbed the armrests and with effort eased back into his chair. I looked around and lowered myself onto the couch, perching on the front edge.

"That's really between Mrs. Grey and me."

"There is nothing between you and the Baroness." He sipped his tea again.

"April Coyote died yesterday," I said. "My mother watched her."

Montgomery offered no sign that this statement merited a response or even that he'd heard me.

"She died saying Mrs. Grey's name." The lie surprised me when it slipped out. "In her journal, she had several references to Vanessa Grey"—I watched for any reaction from the lawyer—"and to my mother's connection with the Grey family. I know April Coyote was here."

"A moment of weakness on my client's part," the

lawyer said. "Security should never have allowed the woman in here. The Baroness should never have subjected herself to the woman's harassment."

I tried to mask my surprise by studying the plush rug at my feet. I'd meant Coyote was here at the club, not the Grey mansion.

"Baroness Grey is not in the best health," Montgomery said. "That woman's visit and your own inquiries have upset her. I think it's time for you to leave—"

"Not yet, Harlan," a raspy voice interrupted. It came from behind Montgomery, from the shadowed portal. An ancient woman came out of the shadows, a nurse guiding her wheelchair until it stopped near Montgomery.

The old crone wore all black. A fleece blanket covered her from the waist down. Makeup gave her face false color, as did gold earrings and a necklace that dangled below her wrinkled neck.

She leaned forward, peered at me and raised one eyebrow in what I took for surprise.

"Closer, Helen," commanded the woman. "I want a better look."

The nurse pushed the wheelchair until the side touched my knees. I started to stand.

"Sit," Grey ordered.

She studied me like I was some kind of exhibit, then raised a hand, and I thought she was going to touch me. Instead, she waved a dismissal.

"That Indian didn't get a penny from us, and now I don't have to give you anything, either," she said. "Stupid. Just like your father."

She laughed. At least, I thought it was a laugh. It sounded more like she was trying to clear phlegm, and soon the noise deteriorated into a coughing spasm. I cringed and leaned back when her spit sprayed my arm.

When she could breathe again, the old lady pointed a bony finger at my chest and croaked, "Get out of my house."

The nurse turned the wheelchair and bumped me with the back wheel.

"Excuse me," she said, and she reached down to pat my knee. She lingered a moment and pressed something into my hand. Then she turned back to the chair, pushing the Baroness past the lawyer and through the opening.

I squeezed the small lump and stared at the shadowy doorway until I felt the security guard's hand on my arm. I stood and saw the lawyer was standing, too.

"What was that all about?" I asked.

"She's ninety-eight," Montgomery said, as if that explained everything. "My advice is that you leave peacefully and forget this evening. It's better that way."

The guard squeezed my arm, accentuating Montgomery's threat.

NINETEEN

I CALLED GINA as soon as I was back in my Bronco and knew I'd be in for it when I heard that Deb had picked up Glory. Then I drove away from Elk Ridge, going about five miles before pulling onto the shoulder. I turned on the overhead light and opened the note.

Whoever had written it—the nurse?—had folded the white paper into an uneven one-inch square. The writing was hasty. A dragging pen tip had connected all the words and numbers.

"EA Wright, 10:15 a.m."

EA Wright and Sons is a medical-supply store in Apostle Bay. The place sells wheelchairs, walkers, oxygen tanks and other hospital equipment. I've never visited the store, but my father mentioned it from time to time.

I guess I'd be checking it out tomorrow morning.

AT HOME I OFFERED a guilty "Hey" when I stepped into the kitchen and girded myself for the complaint I knew was coming.

Deb glanced at me, then she turned back to the sink and continued rinsing dishes as if I'd just returned from picking up milk. Maybe I was off the hook.

Through the wall I heard Glory laughing. I started toward the coat closet, then stopped when I heard a man's voice. Glory squealed with laughter.

"Who's with Glory?"

"Tony. He asked if he could read her the bedtime stories tonight. I didn't have the energy and told him to go ahead. Glory was difficult today, and I needed the break. You weren't much help in the matter. When are you going to stay home two nights in a row? What are you going to do when she's in daycare? Keep pawning her off on people every night when I'm working or at a meeting?"

"What is Tony doing here? I thought you were at yoga tonight. Don't tell me he's in your class."

"I was. He's not, though the studio is open to the public. We don't exclude people on the basis of your mood."

"Nice," I said.

"After class I called Gina and found out you were late—though she tried to cover for you. Tony stopped by to deliver some papers about fifteen minutes ago. I invited him in. Glory was bouncing off the walls, and I didn't look forward to an evening alone with her, thank you very much."

"I'm sorry. I was on an interview at Elk Ridge. They think the rest of the world works on their time."

"But you don't. When are you going to learn that you're a parent? You work on Glory's time."

The house grew quiet.

"Keep it down, Deb."

"Why? Why are you worried what other people think but not worried what Glory or I think?"

"It was important, Deb. This is about family. There is some connection between the woman who died, Vanessa Grey, and my mother. I'm trying to figure out what it is."

"Who cares?" Deb turned off the water, grabbed a towel and turned to face me. "The woman is dead. It's yesterday's news."

She fled the room before I could reply. I stared after her for a moment, then walked out the back door.

OUTSIDE I BLEW OUT a long, frosty breath and watched the moon drifting behind some clouds. Although it wasn't yet September, temperatures were dipping near freezing on some nights and a few leaves had dropped. They crunched as I wandered around the house corner and toward the front yard. I kept walking until I reached Wittmer's car, some kind of fancy, foreign job parked in the street, and bent down to look in the windows. Then I felt guilty about spying. I leaned against the passenger door and waited for Wittmer, wondering again why he'd moved here to Apostle Bay a few years after us. I'd known him as a brief acquaintance in Grand Rapids, where he taught with Deb, and I thought she'd barely known him, too. His arrival here was starting to seem more than coincidence to me.

Five minutes later, the front door of my house opened and Wittmer let himself out. I waited until he was within ten feet.

"Tony."

The man—he had about six inches on me—stopped and flinched.

"You startled me," he said.

"Sorry," I said. It was a lie. I wasn't sorry. "Dropping off some papers?"

"Hmm. Oh, yeah. Bargaining stuff. I'm glad Deb's on the committee. She knows how to cut to the chase when talking with the board."

"Yeah, she's always been good at that. Like tonight with me. I suppose you heard."

"I wish I hadn't."

"You seem to have a way with my daughter. I can't get her to laugh like that."

"Just act like a kid. That works all the time. I have to go."

I didn't move away from the car. "You've been spending a lot of time with Deb."

"We work together."

"Why did you move here? Why, exactly, did you leave a good thing in Grand Rapids?"

"Maybe it wasn't such a good thing."

"Why here? Why follow Deb?"

"I was looking for a job. Deb said Bay High was a good school, and she was right. That's about it. And it's really none of your business."

"I'm making it my business because you answer our phone and read bedtime stories to my daughter. Since you moved here, you spend more time in my house than I do."

"That sounds more like your problem than mine."

"Listen here, Wittmer—"

"If you're suggesting there's something more to our friendship, then you're mistaken. Deb loves you, though I can't see why. You're a lucky guy in two ways: You have both Deb and Glory. Yet, for some strange reason, you're doing your best to blow it."

Tony walked around to the driver's side and opened the door. "I have to get home," he said. He lowered himself into the seat. I pushed away from the car as the engine rumbled and walked back to the house.

TWENTY

I OVERSLEPT THE NEXT MORNING and things started off about as badly as they ended the night before. At city hall I shoved half a grape Pop-Tarts into my mouth while still in the parking lot and decided against calling Lou, hoping the police log would give me a good excuse for arriving late.

I climbed the steps to the police station two at a time, entered the lobby and slowed when I came in sight of the convex mirror. I knew the clerk could see me approach and she buzzed me through the glass security door.

"Morning, Gail," I said to the force's high-energy toothpick who wins almost every road-running and cross-country-skiing race in the region. I walked past her desk toward the dispatch center.

"Hi, Vince," she said in her husky voice, a symptom, I'm sure, of all her cold-weather training. "The chief wants to see you." She lifted her arm and made a point of looking at her watch. "Not like you to be late. Come across a big story on your way to work?"

"If I did, you'd already know about it," I said. I kept heading toward the dispatch center. "I'll check the log, then see the chief."

"Better see him first," she said. "He's been out here twice this morning looking for you."

I spun on my heel and headed to his office. Behind me I heard her pick up the phone and say, "He's on the way back."

The chief's spotless office hasn't changed since my childhood visits. The same pictures decorated the wall: The chief and my father at a Packers game, the chief and Dad in Korea, the chief shaking hands with his predecessor. The desk was the same avocado-green metal, with the same wooden pen holder. The chief even sat in the same worn leather chair that he'd moved from his detective's office.

"Hi, Chief. What's up."

"Have a seat. Coffee?"

"No thanks. I'm kind of in a hurry."

"Well, I wanted to give you a heads up on something, but if you're short of time…"

I sat and tried hard not to roll my eyes. The chief didn't give tips to anyone, and this was, no doubt, another attempt to distract me or give me another lecture.

"Sorry, Chief. What do you have?"

"Gordon tells me you're interested in the small marijuana epidemic we're having."

"I don't know if I'd call it an epidemic, but yeah, I'm curious."

"We have a lead. If things pan out, we may have a break tomorrow night. Gordon will call you with the details if all goes as planned. You may get to be there for the arrest."

"Are you serious?" I doubt the chief had ever given the media advance notice of an arrest. "What's the catch?"

"No catch. No promises, either."

This was so unlike the chief there had to be a catch. "Thanks for the tip. Anyone I know going down?"

"You'll learn more when we're ready. Be patient."

"Sure. Thanks again." I grabbed the chair arms and pushed myself up. "Is that it, Chief?"

Godfather leaned back, folded his arms across his chest and gave me his best fatherly smile. I settled back into the seat.

"I heard you met Vanessa Grey last night."

I dropped back into the chair. "News travels fast."

"She has a nice place. That was your first time there, right?"

"Yes, and nice is not the right word to describe that place. How about palatial."

"The place will be deserted in another week," he said. "Just a security force remains after all the visitors go south with the weather. Some men arrive November 15, try to shoot a few deer and then play high-stakes poker. Other than that, they close up shop until mid-June. Your dad and I used to go on calls there, you know. That was back when the security wasn't high-tech and they didn't have their own medical staff. Most of the time they had more problems than our little town—guys shooting themselves in the foot while cleaning their rifle, kids overdosing on some crazy stuff, runaways lost in the woods. It made me think that their money didn't solve their problems. What did Mrs. Grey have to say?"

"You could have asked me that in the first place," I said. He held the fatherly smile, though I'm sure it was giving him a headache. "It was an odd meeting. The old lady studied me real close—she must have bad eyesight, because she got right up in my face. Then she acted kind of crazy."

"Crazy?"

"Yeah, strange. Did you know that April Coyote met with her also?"

"Their security office said Coyote didn't get past the fence, but Archie was skeptical after spending some time in the car with her."

And since you read the journal, I thought. "Vanessa Grey's lawyer said she's making a habit of talking to people this week. Anyway, she said something about not giving April Coyote any money and not giving me any money, either. Not that I asked for it. Then she called me as stupid as Dad. Her lawyer implied she's going senile. She's closing in on triple digits, you know."

The chief leaned forward, still trying to present the creepy concerned-father smile, but I could tell something had changed. He seemed tired, resigned now.

"So, are you going to pass this on to Mom, Chief? Or should I do it myself?"

"Loretta is worried about you. She's the one who saw the woman die, but it seems as if you're the one trying to make sense out of it. She's trying to forget it. Why can't you?"

I shrugged and stood.

"You inherited your father's stubborn streak," Weathers said. "Sometimes, when we were at a car accident, or even during the war, I think he tried to bring the dead back to life. He never could, you know. You can't, either."

TWENTY-ONE

When I made it to the *Chronicle,* I hid behind my computer, for some strange reason believing this would protect me from Lou's wrath. I'd committed the cardinal sin of missing his editorial meeting.

The morning meetings were rapid-fire planning sessions. Lou drilled each reporter about their work, often injecting a heavy dose of sarcasm, made morning assignments and decided the paper's layout.

I enjoyed the meetings—unless I was the one under scrutiny. I especially liked the last few minutes of each session, which Lou called his "rumor mill." He'd point around the room and ask each person, including administrative and advertising staff that he'd invited to join us, to throw out a piece of gossip—anything they'd heard in diners, on the street, at the party-store checkout. The source didn't matter. Most of these tidbits were slanderous, nothing more than juicy rumor. Some, however, turned into our best stories.

I peeked past my computer and watched Maki arguing with Lou. I caught the words "could be a good story if" from Lou. Maki threw up his hands, returned to his desk and swatted the computer monitor with his notebook.

"What's up, Mort?"

"Teacher contract. Lou complained I wasn't getting anything, so I give him something good and it's not good enough. It's never enough with him."

"Are they close to settling?"

"As if you don't know. I'm sure Deb has told you about the strike."

"Come again?"

"The teachers have threatened to walk. You can read all about it, if I can get someone to answer my calls."

"Vince!" Lou shouted.

I grabbed my reporter's notebook and duckwalked my chair over to Lou's desk.

"Is the police coffee so good you can't pull yourself away to attend our morning meeting?" he said through teeth clenching a pencil.

"No. I didn't have a cup this morning. Hope someone here brewed a fresh pot before things turned busy." Lou didn't smile. "Sorry about the meeting. The chief cornered me and I couldn't get away. However, it may be worth it. They're making progress on the drug investigation and he thinks something's going down tomorrow. They may nail the source. I'll get to be there when it happens."

Kendricks grunted. "I'll believe it when I see it. You have a cell phone. Use it next time."

"I will."

"I hear you've been visiting royalty," Kendricks said. He removed the pencil to jot something on a pad. "How is the Baroness?"

That must have been Gina's contribution to the rumor mill. I was tempted to shoot her a nasty glance.

"I don't think I can tell you without being sued," I said. Lou grunted again. This time I took it for a laugh.

"Are you still digging into the suicide?"

"Might be," I said.

"Is this some kind of personal mission, or is there a story here I'm not aware of?"

"I don't know yet."

"Then work it on your own time. We have a newspaper to put out."

"Fax coming in for you, Vince!" Gina yelled.

"I mean it," Lou said.

"Whoa, this is good," Gina added.

I rolled over and she handed me a page straight from the machine's teeth. It was a restraining order, barring me from any contact with Elk Ridge Hunt and Fish Club members or employees. It was executed this morning by Superior County Circuit Court Judge Dexter Sorenson.

I looked at my watch. Judge Sorenson must have still been in pajamas when he signed that order.

TWENTY-TWO

EA Wright and Sons opened at ten, so I made up some excuse about having an interview and bailed out of the *Chronicle*. I pulled into the parking lot fifteen minutes early and studied the store's small window display. Bamboo and aluminum canes, arranged by length, rested against a pegboard background. A place that sells prostheses and respirators must not need glitzy advertising to draw window shoppers, I decided.

A bald, five-foot-two Yoda without the green skin came to the door and flipped the closed sign to open. He unlocked the glass entrance and signaled me to come inside.

Puzzled, I went into the shop and called out, "Hi."

A string of silver bells hanging from the handle clattered as the door closed. Big-band music, piped through tinny speakers, filled the room. The man stood behind a glass counter filled with various braces and slings. He conducted an unseen orchestra with a red stir straw and a stainless-steel mug.

"Good morning. Good morning. You are Vince Marshall, no? I knew your father well," the man said. "A good man and a good doctor. He liked to say he was going to put me out of business with his doctoring. But alas, they all want to do that and never can. And that's good for me and for my five kids, who all decided they were too uppity for a state college. I'm glad to meet Doc's son."

The old man kept swinging the stir stick but set down his cup and offered his hand. I walked to the counter, reached over and shook.

"Are you EA Wright?"

"Junior. Well, not really junior. My father, Edgar Allen Wright, started this business. Named after Poe. He was, not me. He hated it and really thought the name was bad for a medical-supply business. You know, death and all being associated with Poe. That's why he named the business EA.

"From the day I was born the old man expected me to take over. So I had to have the initials EA but not Edgar Allen. As I said, he hated that. No, Elmer Alfred, that's me. Elmer, can you believe that? Well, none of my kids' names start with E. We'll make a new sign if they ever decide to get in the business, but they all say they're not interested, and that's okay by me, too. Coffee?"

"Sure. You knew my dad?"

"Quite well. He delivered all my children. Betty, that's my dearly departed—two years ago next month— thought Doc was a saint. You don't look much like him, I have to say. Must have inherited your mom's good looks. Lucky for you. Just kidding. By the way, I read your stuff all the time, right after I do the crossword and the Jumble."

"I appreciate that, I think."

"Meant as a compliment. Now, how about you follow me into the back room here for a cup of coffee? Helen will be here in a few minutes. She'll want to talk to you in the back, out of her driver's sight—if you know what I mean."

"How…?"

"She arranged it with me yesterday. After she learned you were going to visit the Baroness. Helen is a good customer of mine, a friend, too. Indeed, I'd never tell anyone, but a good chunk of my business, big-ticket items, comes from the club. And don't print that in the paper."

Wright smiled and tugged me past a curtain into a combination office and kitchen. I noticed an old typewriter on the gray metal desk, and no computer.

Wright continued, "Helen, now there's another lady who thinks your dad walked on water. He sure had a way with the gentler sex. Of course, he saved her son's life, twice, back in the old days when they didn't have staff doctors at the club. Helen's son, well, to be quite frank, he had a problem with the drugs and he got into something bad. It just about killed him. Doc pulled him back from God, or the devil, or whoever was tugging at him from the other side of that bright light people always say they see when they're on the edge. Then Doc got him into a rehab program by calling some buddy from medical school. And somehow he kept everything on the QT so Helen didn't lose her job in the mix."

The bell on the door jangled. Wright put a hand on my arm.

"Stay here now. If that's Helen, I'll bring her back in a few minutes. I don't know what she wants to tell you, but she said she owes something to your dad."

TWENTY-THREE

HELEN WALKED THROUGH the curtain, peeked around the cloth back into the store briefly, then turned and stared at me.

"Hi," I said. I was getting tired of everyone studying me like I was some kind of oddball. "Is something wrong? My collar sticking up? My eye twitching?"

"What?" she asked, looking confused.

"You were staring at me in an odd way, that's all. What can I do for you?"

"Thanks for coming," she said quietly, almost a whisper. The voice went with her looks—bland, like someone used to disappearing into the background. "Elmer told you about my son? How Doc helped?"

"I'm learning a lot about my father these days."

"I was sorry to hear about his death."

"Thanks. So why the clandestine meeting? Surely not to tell me you're sorry about a man who died six years ago."

"I did want to say I'm sorry. I also want to make sure you knew about your dad. About what he did for someone he hardly knew. And I needed to let you know he'd never kill anyone, no matter what the Baroness says."

"Come again?"

"I don't have much time. A security officer drives me here. They're not really watching me, but if the Baroness knew I was talking with you, she'd…well, I don't know what she'd do, but it wouldn't be pleasant."

"And I'd be arrested. The court issued a restraining order against me today. I can't speak to any Elk Ridge staff or residents."

"I saw the Indian girl," Helen said. I needed a moment to realize she was talking about April Coyote. "When the Baroness heard she'd been detained by the guards, she told them to bring that woman to the house. She insisted on it. I don't know why. Just pure wickedness, I guess. As soon as they got together, they both started shouting, as if they knew each other. I've never seen that woman before, and I've been with Baroness Grey for almost twenty years. She, the Baroness, made the guards restrain the woman and silence her." Helen winced as if reliving the moment.

"What was it all about?"

"It was about the Indian woman's sister." Helen looked over her shoulder at the curtain, apparently worried someone might come through at any moment. "The Baroness said that Doc killed her sister. She even said she was glad he did it. She's cruel some, no, most of the time." Her voice trailed off as she said this, and I suspected she'd taken the brunt of that cruelty over the years. "Then she said your father was responsible for what happened to the child, too. I knew none of it was true. Your father couldn't do something like that, but the Baroness said it."

"What are you talking about?"

Helen glanced over her shoulder again and turned partway toward the curtain. "She told that woman your father was dead but your mother was still living in Apostle Bay. She gave her your mother's name."

Helen started backing away.

"What? I don't understand. You have to tell me more."

"I don't know anything else," Helen said. She started through the curtain. "Really, I don't."

I crossed the room, grabbed her wrist as she moved through the curtain and pulled her back.

"That's it? Why would my father kill someone?"

"He wouldn't," she said, trying to twist free. "That's what I'm telling you. He wouldn't. I have to go. I don't know anything else, but I know Doc couldn't have killed anyone."

I released her and stumbled back against the desk, wondering what was going on.

TWENTY-FOUR

MOM DIDN'T SEEM SURPRISED to see me. She opened the door and left me standing in the entrance, telling me over her shoulder that she and Glory were cooking in the kitchen. I followed her and found Glory on the kitchen floor amid pots, pans and wooden spoons. The moment Glory saw me, her top lip started trembling. Tears welled in her dark eyes.

"How nice," I said.

Mom squatted down to Glory's eye level and told her, "Your daddy came to see Nana. Keep playing, sweetheart. Can you bake Nana a cake?" She looked up and added, "Why don't you join us, Daddy?"

"We need to talk alone. Let's get a video going for Glory."

Mom frowned, looked as if she was going to argue, then threw up her hands.

"Let's take some pans into the living room and watch a movie," she said.

I filled Mom's kettle and turned on the burner. While listening to a burst of static and then some Disney theme song, I found two mugs and tea bags. Mom came back into the kitchen as I set the mugs and a sugar bowl on the table.

"I'm not going to tell you how to raise your daughter—"

"But—"

"But a television isn't a baby-sitter."

"No, it's a tool so we can have an uninterrupted discussion about something Glory doesn't need to hear."

"Not that again. Why can't you drop it?"

"Do you know anyone named Helen? Someone Dad helped years ago when her son had a drug problem?"

"Your father helped a lot of people. He would've given the shirt off his back for everyone in this town if I'd let him."

"C'mon, Mom."

She lowered herself into a kitchen chair. "No. I don't remember a Helen."

"She's Vanessa Grey's private nurse."

Mom's shoulders drooped. It was slight, as if her cotton blouse had just grown heavier. The kettle whistled. I turned the stove off and poured hot water into our mugs.

"She told me why April Coyote confronted you at Eagle's Cliff."

I paused, waiting for Mother's reaction. She stirred her tea and didn't look at me.

"Vanessa Grey told April that Dad killed her sister."

"That's not true!" For an instant I saw the mother I was used to seeing: Feisty and confident. Then it faded and she returned to stirring her tea.

As far back as I could remember, Mom had never shied from a fight. Indeed, that's how she met Dad in St. Mark's emergency room after a woman's league hockey game got a little rough. Doc stitched her up—the scar is still visible by her left eye. She asked him out on a date. A year later they were married.

Her current behavior baffled me.

"Why would Vanessa Grey say Dad killed someone?" I asked.

"Why didn't you ask her when you were there?"

"I would have if I'd known she was the instigator. Did the chief tell you about my visit?"

Mom ignored the question. "She's wicked. It was her sick idea of a joke."

"That's what Helen said. Now it makes sense that April followed you the other morning."

"I already told you it was something like that."

"Do you remember April's sister?"

I thought I saw her tense. "It would have been thirty years ago," she said, clearly measuring her words. "That's a long time ago."

I sipped my tea, then decided to approach this from a different angle.

"The medical examiner said a head wound killed April Coyote. She didn't drown. His report said bruises covered her arms, like she'd struggled with someone."

Mom pushed her cup toward the center of the table, looked up and crossed her arms.

"I'm not talking about it anymore. You have something more important to worry about—your family. Deb told me what happened last night. What is going on with you?"

"I don't know," I said, caught off guard. "I think Deb's

having an affair." I regretted saying it as soon as the words slipped out.

"Are you out of your mind? She loves you. She's worried about you. You don't know what a precious gift Deb is—Glory, too. You have something other people would pay *any* price to have. Do you hear me?" She waited until our eyes met. "*Any* price."

TWENTY-FIVE

"GLORY, GLORY, BO-BORY, banana-fana, fo-fory, fe, fi, mo-mory, Glor-eee."

I looked in the rearview mirror and hoped Glory would soon nap in her car seat. Instead, she swung her legs to the song and watched my eyes in the rearview mirror.

We were an hour and a half southwest of Apostle Bay, halfway to the Rum River Casino in northern Wisconsin, and my voice was cracking. Every time I quit singing, Glory screeched. The radio didn't soothe her. When I passed her a new toy, she flung it back at me. So I sang.

This was my mother's idea—not going to Wisconsin. She didn't know about that. Her idea had been for me to take the afternoon off and spend time with Glory. A father-and-daughter outing, she'd said. It was time to build the parent-child bond.

I knew she was right. I also knew driving across the Midwest on a wild-goose chase wasn't what she had in mind. Deb thought it was a stupid idea, too. Indeed, she'd been furious when, thirty miles out of town, I'd called her at the school with my cell phone.

"I'm trying to bond with her. Both you and Mom said I need to do more of that."

"Bringing her on a wild-goose chase for work is not what I meant."

"It's not work. I took the afternoon off. I have her as a captive audience—no interruptions." I thought about adding "And I won't come home to find another man reading her bedtime stories" but knew that would make matters much worse. So instead I said, "Maybe I need a captive audience with you, too. Things haven't been going well."

She filled the uncomfortable pause by changing the subject and reminding me we needed to find daycare.

WHEN WE CROSSED the Michigan–Wisconsin border, I stopped at a fast-food joint and let Glory struggle on the lower level of a children's maze. When she refused to come out of the orange, toddler-sized gerbil tunnel, I crawled in to get her and earned a few dirty looks from parents.

At a roadside stop, I changed her diaper. It was ripe. Glory cooperated, a rare occurrence, while I told her a rambling story about three bears named Larry, Moe and Curly.

As we neared the reservation, I told her how the casino got its name from a nearby river called "river of the spirits" in Ojibwa. Fur traders mistranslated the word for spirits, possibly as a joke, and the tannin-stained water became the Rum River.

It was over her head, but she laughed at my phony French explorer accent.

At quarter to five we pulled into the crowded Rum River Casino parking lot. I unstrapped Glory and then headed toward the main entrance.

TWENTY-SIX

THE BRIGHT LIGHTS, ringing bells and general chaos inside mesmerized Glory. Once my eyes adjusted to the neon hot spots, however, I saw the worn carpet and furniture, fingerprints on video poker screens and smoke: A dense, blue fog that hung from the ceiling and swirled as gamblers walked from slot machines to card tables.

The floor manager directed me through a door marked EMPLOYEES ONLY. I carried Glory up a flight of stairs. Casino employees, hustling down to start their shift, passed. I struggled to keep Glory's hands off their satiny Western outfits and wondered at the irony of Native Americans wearing cowboy outfits.

I followed the corridor past an empty employee break lounge to a small reception area and I almost bumped into the cluttered desk of a dark woman dressed in faded blue jeans and a UW Madison sweat shirt. She was talking on the phone, collating papers and reading something on her computer.

Glory squirmed. I set her on the floor. She grabbed a notepad and paper-clip bin off the desk, dumping the paper clips.

"Glory!"

I whispered "Sorry" to the woman, then lifted Glory

away from the desk and bent down on one knee to pick things up.

"Not for touching," I said.

Glory moved within range of the desk again. I held her back and stood with the paper clips. The woman behind the desk had replaced the phone, was smiling and held out a cookie tin full of broken, peeled crayons.

"Here you go," she said.

She handed the box to Glory, who promptly turned it over and dumped the crayons on the floor.

"Glory!"

"Don't worry about it," the lady said. She was still smiling, and she came around the desk and offered Glory a hand. "We'll get those in a minute, girl. Come let me show you what Darlene has in her drawer over here."

Glory took the woman's hand and followed her around the desk. The woman crouched to toddler height, pulled open her bottom drawer and said, "See if there's anything in here that interests you."

Glory rummaged through the drawer, inspecting and discarding toys onto the linoleum. I started to say something, but the lady stood and held her hand up to stop me.

"It's all right," she said. "I have kids in here all the time. Childcare falls through at the last minute and some of the girls bring their kids to work. That's why I keep this drawer stocked. And it gives me an excuse to eat fast food each week."

I doubted she ate much fast food from her figure.

The lady asked Glory, "How old are you? I'm guessing about eighteen months."

"That's right," I said.

"Hard to believe my own little ones were this age once. They've flown the coop now. Your little girl's a dead ringer for my daughter when she was that young."

She must have started young, I thought. On the desk a folded frame held two high-school-looking photos.

"Are those your children?"

"Yes," the woman said and turned the frame toward me. "These photos are old now. My son's twenty-two. He's a security guard here. My daughter's twenty and a senior at UW Madison. She ended up with the brains that bypassed all the rest of us."

Darlene settled back in her chair.

"What can I do for you?"

"I was hoping to see the personnel manager."

"You're looking at her."

"Oh. Sorry. I'm trying to track down some information on an employee. I hope you can help me."

The woman lost her smile. "And you are?"

"My name is Vince Marshall. This is my daughter, Glory."

"We don't release personal information about employees."

"I figured that. I have a bit of a dilemma. See, the employee's name is April Coyote. Well, I'm not really sure she was an employee here."

Darlene's face hadn't eased, but I detected a flicker of curiosity in her eyes.

"She's, um, well, she died in my hometown this week."

I saw Darlene nod slightly, acknowledging she knew

the fact. That meant the police had probably contacted next of kin.

"I drove up from Apostle Bay this afternoon. The police seem to think it was suicide."

Darlene nodded again and still didn't ease her expression.

"Look, I know this is going to sound kind of strange, but my mother witnessed her death. She was the last one who talked with April before she, um, died. I thought if I could find April's family, somehow I could pass on what she said. I just thought someone should know."

I lowered my eyes and saw Glory gnaw on the head of a red plastic Power Ranger.

"Glory, no. Don't put that in your mouth." I reached forward to grab the toy and Glory turned her head away.

"You'll do better if you tell her what to do, instead of what not to do," Darlene said.

I noticed she'd picked up the phone.

"Get me security please."

TWENTY-SEVEN

"This is Darlene. Please send Gary Redwing up here."

"I'm sorry if I've inconvenienced you," I said, sliding off the chair and gathering crayons. "There's no need for security. We'll get out of your hair."

Darlene replaced the receiver, grabbed something from the drawer, and I heard the distinct clicking of a wind-up toy.

"Hey, Miss Glory, watch what this does."

She set a plastic yellow crab on the floor and it scuttled sideways. Glory dropped the Power Ranger and reached for the crab. She picked it up, looked at it and then tried to put it back on its feet again.

Behind us, heavy treads scuffed each stair in slow rhythm, as if the walker was too weary to climb. I looked back to Darlene, who was sitting in her chair again.

"You're not going to find April's family, because she has none," Darlene said. "Her grandfather died about two weeks ago. Heart failure. That's just a fancy way of saying he got old. April took care of him and they were the last of the family. All we can figure around here is that she snapped after his death. Though I have to tell you, she didn't seem like the suicide type to me. She was a bit too mean, too self-centered. I don't mean that in a bad way. I'm just trying to say that she wasn't the type to jump into a lake when something upset her. She was more likely to clobber someone."

Darlene looked past me, acknowledging someone, and I turned to see a rather beefy bouncer leaning against the wall. He wore the casino's security uniform, but it seemed a size too small, or he was a size too big. His longish, uncombed black hair curled over his ears. His whole appearance was that of a boy in a man's body, despite a few wrinkles creasing his weathered face.

"Gary," she said, "this is Vince Marshall. He's from Apostle Bay."

Gary Redwing avoided looking at me. "Is this about April?" he asked.

"Gary's the closest you're going to get to family," she told me. "He and April dated off and on since…since when, Gary? Since you two were in high school?"

"About that," Gary said.

"I guess if anyone deserves to hear what you know, then he's the one. You two can use the break room. I'll keep an eye on your daughter."

Redwing turned and walked away. I nodded at Glory. "Are you sure?"

"We'll have a good time."

I wavered a bit. Darlene clearly had better child-handling skills than me, and Gary Redwing might be my only chance at local information on April. Still, Deb would be furious if she knew I was leaving our daughter with a strange woman in a casino almost three hours from home.

"Go on," she said. "We're right down the hall. Now go."

TWENTY-EIGHT

In the lounge, Redwing relaxed against the far wall, one dusty boot across the other. The way he settled in, I think he leaned on that wall a lot, had maybe worn a groove or soft spot that fit his expansive shoulders and rounded back. He jammed his left hand into his pocket, and with his right he lit the cigarette hanging from his lips. He ignored me and instead, between hits, studied the smoke curling toward the ceiling.

I got the feeling we'd be there all night if I waited for him to start the conversation, so I ran through my spiel again, already losing hope that I'd learn much from this excursion. Redwing didn't seem interested.

"I knew she was going there," Redwing replied. "She was looking for money. It's all 'cause of those papers she found in her granddad's stuff after he died."

I'd figured she was after money because of what Vanessa Grey had said, but Redwing surprised me by going right to it, not seeming embarrassed about it. I asked if he knew who April was going to see.

"I don't really know. April had some plan, something to do with her little sister, Autumn. Autumn left here when they were still in high school. Nobody knew where she went—at least, that's what April thought. Turns out she was wrong."

He sucked on the cigarette and let the smoke ease through his nostrils, then continued, "You see, Autumn wrote to the old man, her granddad, but he kept that to himself. I guess it was all there, in his desk, letters and stuff."

"What about April and Autumn's mom? Didn't she know where her daughter was?"

"She was dead—cancer. And there was no dad in the picture. Granddad Coyote raised those girls."

Redwing pulled his left hand from his pocket and used it as an ashtray. He still hadn't looked at me, just kept studying that cigarette or the growing haze filling the room.

"I think April was jealous," he said. "You know, 'cause her sister had the guts to do it, to get off the rez. But truth is, her leaving was a relief to the old man. Don't mean it in a bad way, just, well…he had his hands full with those two. They were always going at each other."

"When did Autumn leave?"

"High school. She was maybe sixteen, maybe a little older. From what April told me of the letters, it sounds like Autumn hitchhiked around awhile, then got herself a job up your way, cleaning rooms or something. Supposedly her boss, some rich dude, got her pregnant and they married. Not long after, she got herself killed. I'm not sure how April figured that, must have been in the papers, too, but I don't know. She didn't leave them here."

"I'm sorry," I said, wondering if Chief Weathers had

those documents now. "Must have been a shock for April to lose her grandfather, then learn about her sister after all these years."

Redwing shrugged. "Maybe. She didn't seem right after her granddad died, drinking a little harder that usual, but I guess I understand that. She was tough to read, too. April had a plan. That's all I know. She seemed pretty sure of herself when she left here, kind of excited, I'd say. But she didn't want any company. Whatever it was, she was doing it on her own."

He stepped over to the ashtray and dropped the butt in, leaving it to burn out rather than crushing it. Then he brushed the ashes from his palm, lit another cigarette and moved back to the wall.

I asked if he knew how Autumn died.

He shrugged.

"What about the baby?" I asked. "You said Autumn was pregnant."

"Don't know. Probably died with her, but April wouldn't talk about that, about her sister's death." For the first time, his gaze stopped wandering the room and he looked at me. I thought I saw a trace of curiosity in his eyes. "You sure ask a lot of questions, mister. I thought you were gonna tell me something."

"Yeah, sorry. I'm just trying to figure this all out. Like I mentioned, April followed my mom out to Eagle's Cliff, the place she jumped. She believed my mom knew something about Autumn's death and kind of got in her face about it. But my mom didn't know anything, at least nothing she can remember. Anyway, my mom tried to stop her from jumping. But she couldn't."

"I'm not surprised," he said. "Nobody kept April from doing something once she set her mind on it."

He finished the second cigarette and pushed away from the wall.

"What kind of place was it?" he asked.

"Where?"

"Where April did it. What did you call it? Eagle's Cliff."

"It's a big granite cliff overlooking the lake. Pretty place." I realized after it came out that it was a stupid comment considering his girlfriend's death.

Redwing seemed to think about this a minute, then walked past me to the door. He turned back before leaving.

"You know what?" he said. "April would run off every once in a while, when her mind was all wrapped up in something. But she always came back to me after she got things straight in her head. That's what I liked about her. She always came back."

"I'm sorry."

"I have to get back on the floor."

I grabbed a business card from my wallet and handed it to him.

"If you don't mind, I'm going to see what else I can learn about Autumn. Please let me know if you remember anything else or if those letters of April's grandfather turn up."

Redwing studied the card, then looked up with a hint of annoyance.

"A reporter? That's what this is about?"

"No, this is personal. I just want to find out the truth—find out if there really was a connection between Autumn and my mom. I'm doing this on my own time."

Redwing looked doubtful. "There's one thing I don't get," he said. "April was an excellent swimmer, a fish. She loved the water, loved kayaking, fishing, all that stuff. It sure ain't the way I'd have guessed she'd kill herself."

TWENTY-NINE

I ENTERED OUR KITCHEN just shy of 11:00 p.m. with Glory asleep over my shoulder and was surprised to find Deb cleaning dishes at the sink. It looked like a meal for two, best I could judge.

"Hi," she said. "We need to talk."

"Is this about Glory?" I asked, stifling a yawn, not really wanting to go through it again. "We had a good time. I think we may have bonded a little."

"I'm glad. You don't need to drive to Wisconsin to do it. And no, it's not about Glory."

"Let me get her in bed first, okay?" I wanted to put off what I was sure would be another argument.

I carried Glory to her room and lay her in her crib. Carefully I undressed her and changed her diaper. She stirred a little as I bent her legs into a fleece sleeper, but seemed down for the count. I took my time, enjoying a chance to watch her sleeping, savoring the rare quiet moment for us and not really wanting the day I'd had with her to end—not yet.

BACK IN THE KITCHEN, I slumped into a chair, exhausted now from the drive. Deb was finishing at the sink.

"How was dinner?" I asked, noticing a candle still

burning at the table's center and a pair of dessert dishes with some kind of chocolate smeared on them in the open dishwasher. "Looks like the remains of a good meal for two."

"Fine," she said, either not getting my point or ignoring it. She grabbed a newspaper from the counter and dropped it on the table in front of me. It was that day's edition of the *Chronicle*. "We need to talk about this. Why didn't you tell me this was coming?"

The headline above the fold said TEACHERS THREATEN STRIKE.

"Why didn't you tell me you were planning to walk?" I asked.

"Because we're not. The first time I heard about it was when some friends called me today and asked for more details after reading *this* story. Where do you guys get off publishing fiction?"

I thought about defending the *Chronicle* but didn't have the energy.

"Listen, Deb, Mort Maki mentioned something about it this morning, and it didn't sound like it was going to pan out. When I asked him for more details, he told me to talk to you. Then I forgot it. I honestly did."

"Yeah, you're too busy chasing your own myth—"

"Deb, that's not—"

"This story is bogus, Vince. We've never threatened to strike. We've never asked for anything outrageous. All we're trying to do is preserve our benefits and salaries, not go backward. This"—she said, slapping her hand on the paper—"makes it sound like we're a bunch of uncooperative bullies trying to stick it to the community. I can't believe this."

"Let me read it."

I took the paper and skimmed the story. It wasn't as bad as she made it sound, but in a general sense, she was right. Some readers would think the teachers' union was unreasonable, but only because the school board, Ken Romano to be specific, said it was. The teachers' spokesman, Tony Wittmer, offered no comment to balance it, saying that the board and teachers had agreed to keep negotiations private. Wittmer was quoted in the first part of the piece, saying strikes were always a possibility in negotiation.

I dropped the newspaper on the counter.

"I wouldn't worry about it, Deb."

"It turns the public against us."

"I think that was the board's plan. Tell Wittmer to either go all out and answer questions next time so it's more balanced or stick with no comment."

"I don't care that you work there, Vince. Tomorrow I'm calling Mort and giving him an earful. This is just outrageous."

"Don't, Deb. If you do, if you say something out of anger, even one sentence, it'll end up in a story. Look what happened with Wittmer today. That was bone-headed for him to say that thing about striking."

"It was taken out of context," she protested. "Tony never said we were going to strike."

"I'm just saying Maki will key on your emotion and you'll regret it. You're better off letting it ride."

"Are you telling me that you write that way, Mr. Always-searching-for-the-truth? Do you take emotional comments and twist them to serve your purpose?"

I sighed. "I wouldn't call it that. Maybe—"

I held up my hand to stop her interruption.

"Maybe Mort asked him a leading question. And maybe he used the answer out of context. But if a person is stupid enough to say it, then maybe the public should hear that they can't contain their emotions. Especially when it's a public issue. And in situations where the facts are being kept confidential—and unless I'm mistaken, you can't talk about the contract details—there's not much else to put in the story but emotional comments, people's opinions. Maki's under pressure to produce and he doesn't have anything. Don't give him something."

"It's not fair."

"It's life. Don't let the school board pressure you with this tactic. It plays right into their hands. People will forget this in a day or two." I stifled another yawn and pushed back from the table.

"I don't think they will. And I don't like the idea of not responding."

"Sometimes it's the best thing to do. C'mon, Deb. It's late. I'm going to bed."

"Not me. I'm too wired for sleep."

I couldn't help wondering if she really was too jazzed or if it had something to do with the dinner guest I suspect had left not long before we returned. But I was too tired to head down that road tonight.

THIRTY

MY CELL PHONE RANG while I was still in the driveway the next morning. Seeing the *Chronicle* on the caller ID was a surprise.

"Is that you, Lou?"

"Yeah. Jack Stevens from the AP called," Kendricks said. "Vanessa Grey's batteries ran out of juice last night."

"She died?"

"Bingo. He's looking for background on Vanessa Grey and Elk Ridge."

"Send him to the historical society." Stevens covered Michigan's Upper Peninsula for the Associated Press. In my mind he was the competition, even if we were paying for his services. "How'd the AP find out before us?"

"Her public-relations flunkies are falling all over themselves to memorialize her," Kendricks said. "Listen, Vince, since you were there two days ago, I want to take advantage of it. Check with the cops. See if they've heard anything. Then get over to the historical society and see what you can get from Patrice—I've arranged for her to meet you there."

I groaned. The last person I wanted to visit this morning was the historical society's anal-retentive archivist,

Patrice Berklee. She was the sole person in control of
Apostle Bay's ancient documents—items she guarded
with an unyielding mania.

Lou had struck up a relationship with her soon after
buying the *Chronicle*. Indeed, he did it as soon as he'd
learned the previous managing editor, in a foolish effort to clean house, gave all the *Chronicle*'s back issues
and microfilms to the Society. We didn't have a scrap of
evidence within our building that the newspaper existed
prior to four years ago. After Kendricks had finished
cursing the man, he'd courted Patrice, a retired history
professor from Michigan State. Now, on the rare occa-
sions he actually left our building, he was one of the few
allowed into her document vault.

"Be here by nine with background and a feature you
can write, including perspectives from your visit," Kendricks added. "I want to know what the house was like,
what she looked like, her health, whatever. You know
the drill."

AT THE POLICE STATION, I checked the overnight log. There
were a few drunk-driving stops and a vandalism complaint at Romano Auto Sales that caught my eye. Someone smashed the showroom window and spray painted
cars on the lot. I made a note to call Romano, then realized I'd never get to it this morning if I had to see Patrice. I called Lou.

"Are you at the historical society yet?" Kendricks
yelled.

"Lou, I just arrived at city hall. Vandals nailed

Romano Auto Sales last night—sounds serious. I think you ought to send a photographer to get some pics and maybe have Mort look into it."

"You're making assignments now?"

"You want me to handle it and let Maki deal with Patrice Berklee?"

"No, that won't do. How bad was it?"

"The report says the showroom windows were smashed and a bunch of new cars were decorated with blaze-orange spray paint."

"You think there's any way it's related to the school-board mess? Some kind of retaliation?"

"Anything's possible," I said but hoped for Deb's sake it wouldn't be a teacher. "A witness claims she saw a jacked-up cherry-red pickup cruising near the dealership early this morning. She was on her way home from work at the hospital and said the driver was acting suspiciously. That's all the cops have so far, but I'm guessing they'll check the school's parking-permit list for any employees with a red truck."

"I'll get Maki on it when he arrives," Kendricks said. "What about Elk Ridge? Did they call for an ambulance last night?"

"No. There's nothing from dispatch, but they have their own doc, so that's not a surprise."

"Then get over to the museum. Patrice is probably waiting for you."

I heard a click, pocketed my phone and stuck my head into Greenleaf's office.

"Gordo, you've been hiding on me. What can you tell me about Vanessa Grey's death last night?"

I saw the surprised look I'd expected.

"What are you talking about?"

"The Baroness. She kicked the bucket last night. I guess that makes me a suspect, since I was there two days ago and they filed a restraining order against me."

"That's odd. The chief was there yesterday." It was my turn for surprise. "The Eagle's Cliff jumper tried to get in there a few days ago, too."

"Not try—she got in." I told Greenleaf about my visit to the club. "What was the chief doing there?"

"I don't know, and I didn't ask. The only reason I know he was there is that I saw his car pull out of the access road when I was heading north yesterday afternoon. I heard you were in Wisconsin."

"I hate small towns. Who told you?"

"Deb. Did you learn anything interesting?"

I gave him an abbreviated version of the trip, skipping the reservations Darlene and Redwing had about April's suicide.

"I guess that explains why she was in Apostle Bay," Greenleaf said.

"Yep."

"Are you going to keep digging on this?"

"Yep."

"Gonna let me know what you find?"

"Sure. Let me know what you hear about Vanessa Grey. I have to put a story together this morning. Any news on the drug bust tonight?"

"Nothing against you, Vince, but having the media there is a bad idea. I don't know what got into the chief's head. He's been acting odd this week."

"He thinks he's distracting me from April Coyote. And don't try too hard to talk him out of it, Gord. I deserve a break once in a while."

"No, you don't." Greenleaf paused, picking up his pencil and tapping it on the desk calendar the way he did when he wanted to ask me something.

"What is it, Gord?"

"Something you said the other day made me curious."

"So you *were* listening."

"You have time to talk about it?"

"Not now. How about lunch? The Laughing Whitefish around noon?" I pushed away from the door. "I want to visit the chief before I leave and see what he was doing at Elk Ridge yesterday. And Patrice Berklee is probably going to ban me from the historical documents if I make her wait much more."

"Forget what I said about the chief," Greenleaf said. "I shouldn't have mentioned it. You didn't hear me mention it—got that? Besides, he's not here this morning."

THIRTY-ONE

The Apostle Bay Historical Museum occupies the premier downtown building: A former bank on the corner of Main overlooking the lake. The local historical society renovated the bank's lobby, with its twenty-foot-high ceiling and ornate woodwork, to make exhibit areas. The two-level fire-safe vault became the document repository.

To Patrice Berklee, who preferred the company of musty, yellowed newspapers and other documents to people, the vault was a shrine.

I pulled into an alley one block south of Main and parked by the building's rear entrance. Patrice was waiting beside her gray Subaru wagon, staring at me like I was late and troublesome. She looked as she always did, clad in black, mourning the present.

I got along as well as one can with Patrice, frankly, because my dead father fascinated her. She believed Doc would have been a great source of local history because he had contact with so many townspeople. She was always on my case to turn over his files and notes to the museum. I hadn't told her that was under Mom's control, not mine, since I was hoping to keep parlaying her interest into cooperation.

"Thanks for helping us," I said, struggling to keep up as she unlocked the door. She frowned over her shoulder and told me she wasn't happy to be there. I also knew, however, that she was curious about the Grey family. I told her about my visit to Elk Ridge two days earlier as we wound our way past a life-size diorama of early Native American life on Superior's shore.

"You were in the club? Tell me. No, wait. I know how you'll pay back the favor you owe me for this early-morning call. I want you back this afternoon. I want to record your impressions, today, while they're fresh, everything you saw, heard and smelled. Everything."

ONCE INSIDE the document-viewing room, she told me to park my fanny at a conference table and put on a pair of white cotton gloves, required of any person who might touch one of her documents, while she unlocked and pulled open the massive circular door. Patrice strode onto the vault's catwalk, her feet ringing on the metal, and disappeared down a circular stair to the lower chamber, where all the safety-deposit boxes had been removed and replaced with document-storage drawers. I could hear her rummaging around, rolling open and banging closed metal cabinets.

"Ah, here's what I wanted," she said, her voice echoing on the vault's walls. She climbed the stair, came out and placed three binders on the table in front of me. Inside the books were plastic sleeves holding news clippings.

"This is the Grey file," she said. "It's mainly news

stories about mining. I'll see what I have on life at Elk Ridge next."

I looked at the three fat books and then at my watch.

"Uh, Patrice, I need to be at the office in twenty minutes with enough background to whip out a story. And I'll have only a half-hour to do that. I know it's not your preferred method, but any chance you could give me a quick synopsis?"

Patrice glared.

I gave her my best beleaguered look and added a plaintive "Please."

"I suppose it's either that or have to suffer through a hack job full of error and misinformation," she said. "What do you need?"

"A brief history of the Grey family and Elk Ridge."

"In fifteen minutes or less," she said with her usual dose of sarcasm.

"Exactly."

As if she'd returned to a lecture hall in East Lansing, she paced the area in front of my table and briefed me while I took notes on the laptop.

Vanessa Grey was the daughter of Baron William Peter Grey and Lady Regis Grey. The Baron was born in Wales with a title, a castle, a small tin mine and no money, thanks to his father, who gambled away the family fortune. His greatest assets, it turned out, were a knowledge of mining processes and a sense of timing.

Iron was already a big business in Northern Michigan and Minnesota, with more than a hundred operating mines in the region when Baron Grey came to the

States to get a piece of the action. The first mine opera-
tors were land speculators, entrepreneurs with business
knowledge but no clue about ore extraction or geology.
Early mines were crude operations. Grey saw this and
traded his know-how for a partnership in two mines on
the range. He brought order and efficiency, first to the
extraction process, later to methods of processing the
ore. Grey undersold his competitors and then bought
them off until he owned what geologists refer to as the
entire Huron Iron Range, a body of iron deposits cen-
tered in Michigan's Upper Peninsula.

As the First World War approached, and at the same
time the automotive industry was taking off, Grey knew
demand for iron and steel was about to skyrocket. He
expanded operations to include steel mills in Detroit and
Chicago. Part of that deal was the marriage of Vanessa
to Rochester Pontcliff, son of a financier who helped
fund his first Great Lakes plant.

Grey Industries moved its center of operations to
Chicago in 1920. William Grey, however, maintained
a fondness for his northern wilderness. He established
the Elk Ridge Hunt and Fish Club in 1923 as a place to
mimic the royal hunt clubs in his home country. He invited business partners, bankers and other industrial-
ists to join, and they gladly did for an outrageous fee.

Vanessa and her new husband spent summers at Elk
Ridge and winters at Grey's castle in Wales—the Elk
Ridge version is a replica—where Rochester sired two
children and drank profuse amounts of gin.

William Grey fell in love with his adopted country

and never returned to the UK. When he died in 1938, Vanessa left Rochester in Wales and returned to Chicago to manage the company. She insisted on the title Baroness and the name Grey. She never returned to her husband, indeed, never used his name again, and controlled Grey Industries until the late eighties, when her nephew took over as president and CEO.

"You wouldn't happen to know anything about the families that lived there, say, thirty, maybe thirty-five years ago?" I asked. "I've been looking into a rumor someone at the club married a Native American girl who worked there as a maid or cleaning lady. Probably would have been a scandal back then and it might be linked to a recent death."

"Doesn't ring a bell," she said dismissively. "It's unlikely. The families at Elk Ridge would have bought off the woman with a threat and a one-way ticket to somewhere far away. Things were different back then. The woman couldn't go on *Oprah* or something and embarrass the club."

"Thanks," I said, checking my watch. "I've got a few more minutes. Anything else I should know?"

"You don't really want me to answer that."

THIRTY-TWO

CONSIDERING THE NOTICE we had, the Vanessa Grey memorial edition came together well. Patrice found some historical photos, the AP came through with several inches of broad history and the obit, and my piece seemed to earn Lou's grunt of satisfaction.

Soon after the press was rolling, I headed over to the Whitefish Cafe for my meeting with Greenleaf. He proceeded to give me an agrarian lesson on marijuana.

The way Gordon described it, pot-smoking aficionados throughout the United States will pay a premium for a strain called Eden, a tall, potent marijuana plant that grows only in the rural Northern Michigan farming community of the same name.

Eden is a rare agricultural haven, as its name suggests, about fifty miles south of Apostle Bay. Lake Michigan surrounds the narrow strip of land and continues warming it long after the normal growing season for that latitude. The soil is black and fertile, a byproduct of the nitrogen-rich sediment deposited there following the last ice age.

Marijuana is the crop of choice for some in this small peninsula community—no surprise considering the market value compared to potatoes and beans, the region's other cash crops. The rural location and minimal law-enforcement presence also play a part in that equation.

Users pay top dollar for Eden because the strain contains potent levels of tetrahydrocannabinol, the psychoactive chemical in pot. The strain also grows bushy and tall. Farmers can conceal plants within corn rows and know sunlight will still energize the plant.

The farmers in Eden send their product south, not bothering with the small buyers they could find in remote Northern Michigan towns.

"Until now," Greenleaf told me.

"Let me guess: In all the arrests this summer, the kids had Eden weed," I said.

"That's what the state forensic lab says."

A waitress placed our sandwiches—turkey club for me, a Reuben for Greenleaf—on the table. While she refilled our coffee mugs, I watched an ore freighter unloading coal at the city's power plant. The ship would collect a load of iron-ore pellets and head for the Soo Locks by nighttime.

"Green Bay police have an informant," Greenleaf said after the waitress left. "They tell us two gangbangers are coming here to buy a large volume of Eden at cut-rate. Someone local is trying to unload it fast."

"A farmer from the peninsula?"

"We don't think so. Those guys deliver straight to big distributors in Green Bay, Milwaukee and Chicago."

"Who, then? How are the kids involved?"

"I think someone brought in a large load, planned to sell it locally and is having second thoughts. Now they're trying to dump it. Or maybe someone happened upon a stash while visiting Eden—partridge hunting or something—and they decided to get into the trade."

"Is that the person you hope to catch tonight?"

Greenleaf washed down a bite of sandwich with coffee. "We'll get to that in a minute. First, I've been thinking about your wife knowing some of the kids arrested this summer and saying they're good kids. She's right. I looked into it, and they're not only good kids, they're the best kids at Bay High."

"Even the best mess up."

"Eight kids were arrested. I talked with the school principal. They are the top eight students in this year's senior class. Right now they're all vying for valedictorian. Coincidence?"

"It's not a coincidence if they're all buddies who hang out together. Or if they think they're smart enough to start a little side business."

"For the most part, they're not buddies. I checked that, too. Some of them hang with the same crowd, but they can be cutthroat when it comes to class rank. Do you remember any of the arrest details?"

"All the kids were charged with possession. They all held small amounts. I don't think anyone was using or selling. Each kid claimed he or she didn't know they had the stuff. Police found the drugs in beach bags, backpacks, purses, et cetera. The judge slapped the kids' hands—fines and a suspended sentence—except, of course, Ken Junior. He never made it to court, not even a preliminary hearing, thanks to the prosecutor."

"Here's something you don't know because we held it back," Greenleaf said. "In seven of the eight cases, we had an anonymous call that led to the arrest. Romano is the only kid arrested without a tip. One of our officers saw him acting suspicious at the teen center and later caught him holding."

"And he walks."

"Right. Here's why: He claimed he's the anonymous source. I believe him. The kid had the details right. And he says that when he was caught he'd been using the weed as bait. He was trying to determine who else was involved so he could rat on them, too."

"And his dad is in charge of the prosecutor's campaign funds. Go figure."

"And someone vandalized Romano Auto Sales last night. Coincidence?"

"I thought the vandalism was related to the teacher contract, a couple of angry instructors sending the school board a message."

"That's what Romano tells us. I have my doubts."

"Why?"

"Call it instinct. The vandalism was too methodical for a few teachers upset over contract negotiations. Plus, the vehicle someone saw at the scene doesn't match anything on the school's permit list."

That news would gladden Deb's heart, I thought. I looked out the window again. Superior was slate-gray beyond the ore dock, same as the low-hanging clouds. On days like this, you couldn't determine where the water stopped and sky started.

I asked Gord, "Are you saying that Romano, or his kid, framed those other students so Ken could lock in valedictorian?"

"Does it sound that crazy? The principal thinks I'm nuts. But he did say if there's a tie in the grades, the top student is chosen by a committee based on extracurricular activities, community service and moral character. If Romano is the only kid without a record, he's in."

"Why would he risk it?"

"It can mean a lot of extra scholarship dollars," Greenleaf said.

"That's weak. His family doesn't need it. Three-quarters of Apostle Bay residents buy their cars from this guy."

"Even rich people get in money trouble. My gut tells me I'm close."

"Even if you're right, Gord, how does it play into tonight? You think the father or son is trying to unload the stuff?"

Greenleaf shrugged again. "I guess we'll find out. The buy is supposed to happen at the Ramada Inn. We're told the guys coming up from Green Bay will check into a room and wait for contact. I'll have undercover officers at the hotel all day. A couple of sheriff's deputies are helping. If it looks like it's going down, I'll call you. Keep your cell phone handy."

"Are you sure you won't forget in the heat of the moment?"

"I'm sure I'll want to. But I won't."

THIRTY-THREE

THE FLOWERS—bought on my paltry *Chronicle* expense account—barely turned Patrice Berklee's head. Same for the two copies of that day's edition, which I dropped on the conference table.

"The tape machine's set up," Patrice said. "Are you ready?"

"Lou sends his thanks, Patrice. He said he'd call you later and offer his gratitude in person. Great photo of Vanessa christening the ore freighter *William P. Grey*. It ran in Detroit, Chicago and some of the financial dailies—with due credit to the Society."

Patrice snorted. "An ill-fated ship. After you left this morning, I discovered that she sank during her first year on the Great Lakes."

"Nice," I said.

"Let's start. Then I can tell you what I found regarding your other inquiry."

"My other... You found something?"

"After the interview," Berklee said.

She must have been in a good mood. She let me enter her vault for the Q&A.

WHEN PATRICE WAS SATISFIED she'd milked me dry, she turned off the recorder, opened her top desk drawer and pulled out a thin manila folder.

"This is a transcript made by the previous archivist. It's an interview with the former groundskeeper, Ernie Heikkinen. He would have been working at the club around the time you're interested in. Do you remember I said they hired a lot of locals back then? He seems to have been familiar with most of the club families."

"Is he still alive?"

"I don't know. Our director thinks so. He's probably your best bet for any unpublished information and gossip about the Elk Ridge families. If he doesn't know anything, he might have a line on someone else who worked at the club."

"Thanks, Patrice. If this pans out, I'll tell you what I learn."

"If this pans out, I want a look at your father's stuff."

"You have a deal," I said, figuring I'd worry about Mom's opinion on that later.

THIRTY-FOUR

THE PHONE BOOK listed three Ernie Heikkinens. I tried the one listed in Bowling, a small village fifteen miles north of Apostle Bay near the club's property, and hit pay dirt. Ernie's wife told me I'd find her husband drinking coffee at his second home, the Hardees in Apostle Bay.

I checked in with Lou, gave him an update on the drug bust and said I'd be back in the evening to write the story. Then I drove to the fast-food joint.

I FOUND THE FORMER groundskeeper—white-haired and big as a tractor—sitting sideways in a chair, his left armpit over the back, his legs crossed. He wore faded jeans, a black-and-gray wool shirt and grimy, rainbow-striped suspenders.

Heikkinen was drinking coffee and sharing a pile of fries with a shrunken, toothless man who looked like one of those wizened apple heads kids carve at Halloween. They both sat on the window side of the table, facing in toward the customers.

"Vince Marshall the reporter?" Apple Face asked, his voice a nasal, whiny twang. "Any relation to Doc Marshall?"

"His dad, you numbskull." This was Ernie talking.

"The man who took your arm? Jeez, you ain't going to clock him, are you, Ernie?"

"Wasn't his daddy that got my arm. It was the chain saw," Ernie said. He turned to show that his left arm ended four inches below the shoulder.

"Heh, heh, you mean the chain saw and the twelve-pack you had for lunch," said Apple Face.

Ernie glared and I thought for a moment he was going to launch a backhanded swat at his cohort. Instead, he broke into a guffaw and everyone sitting near us looked up to watch.

Ernie grabbed an empty chair from the next table and dragged it over. "Have a seat," he told me. "Get this man a cuppa joe," he yelled to the counter.

"He can get it himself, old-timer," the cashier yelled back. But she'd already grabbed the pot and was reaching for a foam cup. I shook my head no, but when she'd filled the cup, I went to the counter, handed her a buck and took it.

I settled into the chair.

"So, why is a big-shot reporter interested in an old one-armed guy from Bowling?" Heikkinen asked. He and Apple Face had moved to the edge of their seats and I got the impression of two mutts staring at me like I held a dripping steak in one hand. I was probably the most entertainment in their lives in weeks.

"I'm digging into a little rumor I heard about Elk Ridge, something that happened about thirty years ago. You were the groundskeeper then, right?"

"Yep," he said. "Best job I ever had."

"Heh, heh, only job you ever had," said Apple Face. He leaned toward me and stage-whispered, "His daddy was the groundskeeper before him. Kept it in the family."

Heikkinen nodded agreement. "I don't know if I'll be much help. I minded my own business, like I was told. Kept the flowers watered, trees trimmed and cleaned up after a storm or two. It was a good job, like I said. Had any tool I needed, plenty of help."

"Good job if you're a kissup," his partner said. "People up there think you're some kind of lowlife 'cause ya work for a living. They haven't a clue. Heck, I've watched 'em stumble around in their Orvis gear like blind tourists—raw meat for the skeeters and blackflies. Many's the time I had one of those jokers in my sights"—he sighted down an imaginary rifle when he said this—"and coulda plugged 'em with my ought-six. No one would be the wiser."

"Don't pay no mind to him," Heikkinen said. "He got busted trying to sneak lunkers out of the stream on the wrong side of the fence, back when he was spry enough to wade a stream and climb a fence. He hasn't had a kind word since. Truth is, the club was a good place to work. Put my son through junior college thanks to that job. So go on, what's this rumor you're digging into?"

"Do you remember any stories about someone from the club having an affair with one of the maids—a Native American woman?"

"Happened all the time," Heikkinen said. "Some of those old guys had affairs with half the help."

"Sin city, that's what that place is," Apple Face said.

"A den of iniquity. Yep. One time I sat on the hill on the south end of their property. I was stalkin' a 12-pointer, a real beauty, and I saw one them pretty boys—"

"Pay no mind to him," Heikkinen interrupted. "What I was trying to say here, Vince, is that these guys would bring business folks up, take them on a hunt and some of the staff would entertain them, you know, be their dates. I think a couple of them gals saw it as a ticket out of here, a ride to the big city. But the truth is, they was just part of the scenery."

"Just part of the scenery," Apple Face echoed. "Yep, heh, heh, nothin's changed, Ernie. You're still just part of the scenery, 'cept it's the Hardees scenery."

Heikkinen rolled his eyes and grabbed a fry. He pointed it toward me.

"But there was one little Indian girl who caught a big fish," Heikkinen said. "I remember her well 'cause she was the end of a good thing for me and a lot of other folks."

Bingo, I thought.

"Happened in the spring, like you said, probably thirty years back or more. She worked as maid, if I remember right."

"Yeah, trout season," Apple Face said. "That's when all the women and children move up for the summer break. Security tightens so's you can't even cast a line in some of their creeks without getting harassed."

Ernie ignored his friend. "She was a young girl, as I was saying, looked no more than sixteen. Somehow she made friends with William—"

"Vanessa's father?" I asked.

"Nah. He was dead by then. It was the Baroness's son. Just a kid. Probably about twenty. Still in college at some fancy school, from what I heard. Now, I'm just telling you the gossip, 'cause I don't know for sure. They said he got this girl in a family way, if you know what I mean. And the Baroness nearly went mad when she found out. She was going to ship him back to England and send the Indian to one of those clinics. But we heard the kid actually told his mother to stick it 'cause he was going to marry the girl. The Baroness probably said it would be over her dead carcass."

"That old witch," Apple Face said. "She's the worst one."

"How would you know?" Ernie replied. "You've never even been in the club except those times you got caught trespassing. You wouldn't know the Baroness if she was sitting here at this table."

"That old witch, as you called her, died last night," I said. "Did you ever meet her, Ernie?"

"Nah. She passed by me on occasion when I was working outside the castle. I did a lot of work there. But we, the employees, you know, were just like another tree or a pile of brush to them people."

"What happened to her son and the girl?"

"Don't really know," he said and grabbed another fry. He chewed as if recalling his days as the grounds-keeper. "No, I take that back. They ran off. That was the worst of it, what really set the Baroness on a rampage."

"Do you have any idea where they went?"

"Oh, I heard a story. Someone said they saw the girl waiting tables at a tavern west of here, somewhere out near the mines. A place called the something Moose, or Moose something. I don't recall. I doubt she lasted long there. She wasn't too popular in these parts. For all I know, the boy dumped her once his pocket change ran out and he went back to mama."

"I imagine the others were jealous of her," I said.

"Yeah, there was some of that. But the big thing is that girl cost us our jobs. We had a good thing going up there. Come down to it, she's really the one who cost me this, too," he said and waved his stump.

"How so?"

"Once the Baroness ran that girl off, she decided they'd have no more locals working there to tempt the kids. It was okay for the men to play their games, but there'd be no kids fallin' in love. We were all gone by the end of the summer. They brought private staff in, from who knows where, to do our jobs."

"And the arm?"

"Logging accident," Ernie said. "I took to the woods to earn a few bucks after the unemployment ran out."

THIRTY-FIVE

THAT NIGHT THE RAIN came down in sheets and saturated me on the twenty-yard jog from my Bronco to the glass entrance of the Big Boy. I entered a crowded foyer, squeezed through people waiting for the downpour to ease and shed my soaking coat.

Through a haze drifting out of the smoking section, I saw Gordon at the counter, his back to the door and a rain jacket across his knees.

I slid onto the stool next to him.

"Next time you call me out on a night like this, let me borrow one of your wetsuits," I said.

With a handful of napkins from the chrome dispenser, I tried to dry off. Gordon, I noticed, was chuckling.

"Sorry I'm late," I said. "I had to make last-minute arrangements for Glory to stay at Mom's house. She wasn't cooperating."

"Who? Glory or your mom?"

"The kid. I forgot Deb had another meeting tonight. Contract negotiations."

"I hear tempers are a little hot," Greenleaf said. "Are they really going to strike?"

"Who knows? What's going on here?"

Greenleaf nodded toward a booth in the smoking

section without looking that way. In my best spy style, I turned and saw a white kid, late teens, in a Green Bay Packers jacket. A red 'do-rag was wrapped around his head. A dozen black hairs sprouted from his chin. A half-smoked cigarette hung from his lips. The kid held a ketchup bottle in one hand and pounded on it with the other. After each slap to the bottle, cigarette ash dropped onto the kid's plate.

Across the booth, another boy, African-American and probably the same age, chowed a burger. This kid's hair sprang at least a foot above his head. I wondered if it would stay there in the rain.

"These are the drug guys?" I asked. "They're just kids."

"Yep. Except they have rap sheets, guns in their pockets, and they push drugs to even younger kids. Gang leaders like them young. They're impressionable, and they don't stay in jail long, if at all."

"They're carrying? Now?" I looked again, as if I would see a weapon sticking out.

"Sure," Greenleaf said. "Make no mistake, they're kids without a conscience."

Ketchup Boy looked up, caught my eye and I realized I'd been staring at him. He pointed the ketchup bottle at me and curled his lip like a dog showing teeth. I looked away, threw the damp napkins onto the counter, then asked the waitress for coffee.

"How long have they been here?"

"Since I called you. I think they're killing time."

"What's the plan?"

"Wait. When they leave, I follow them," Greenleaf said. "You go to the Ramada—"

"But—"

"No arguments. This is your special look at police work. I should have sent you straight to the Ramada to wait with Lucy, but I was getting bored and wanted company."

"Lucy Demott?" I asked.

"Yeah."

"At least the TV station sent someone with sense," I said. I hadn't cared for our local television reporter Lucy Demott since the day she pulled the old your-fly-is-open trick and then pushed in front of me for an interview with Governor Jennifer Granholm. I did, however, grudgingly respect her. Lucy was canny. She understood the issues, and she usually asked something I forgot to cover in an interview.

"When you get there," Greenleaf continued, "park near a dark green Jeep Cherokee and switch cars. Archie Freeman is sitting in the Jeep, and he's your baby-sitter."

"That clown?"

Greenleaf chuckled.

"Between us, he's been in two car chases this week, *while he was off duty.* Both times the driver thought he was some nut impersonating a police officer, and that's why they split."

"I'm not surprised."

"He's the perfect baby-sitter for you because he's dying for an excuse to hit you with his Taser. So don't so much as think about doing something stupid."

"No problem. I'm Mr. Cooperation."

"Yeah, right." Greenleaf rolled his eyes, then sipped his water. "Be patient, let us do our job, and you'll get plenty of good stuff for tomorrow's *Chronicle*."

"If I'm locked in the Jeep, how do I get to see the action?"

"After everyone's in custody and we have things secure, we'll have a parade in the hotel lobby and you can shoot all the pictures you want. Until things are clear, sit tight and get to know Archie a little better. Who knows, you two may hit it off."

Greenleaf stood and dropped a five on the counter. "Looks like I'm out of here. Give us a head start, then go find Archie."

I nodded, sipped my coffee and saw Ketchup Boy paying at the cash register. The kid fired up another cigarette. Instead of walking toward the exit, he strolled my way. Greenleaf, I knew, was already out the door.

The kid's hand, the one holding the cigarette, landed next to my arm. Blue ink from a homemade tattoo stained his biceps and grime lined his fingernails. I picked up my mug and sipped again, ignoring the smoke he blew past my face.

"Saw you checking me out." The kid leaned close, until his breath, reeking of stale tobacco and fries, coated my neck. He put his lips by my ear and whispered, "I got some cold steel right here in my pocket. You want some of it?"

Before I could think of a response, I saw the kid's arm fly back and he disappeared.

"C'mon, you idiot," I heard another voice, this one deeper, a hint of exasperation in it. "Quit messing around."

"Who you calling an idiot, you idiot?" Ketchup Boy said.

I watched them head out the door, then tried to calm the thumping in my chest.

THIRTY-SIX

"FIGURED IT WOULD be you," Freeman growled when I climbed into the Jeep.

"A howdy-do to you, too," I said and settled into the Jeep's back seat.

"Keep your mouth shut and don't move a muscle," he said.

"I see you two know each other," Lucy Demott said.

"Best of friends," I responded.

Then we sat, silent except for the rain dancing on his SUV, until Freeman resumed a conversation he'd been having with Demott. Apparently he was giving her his life history. Freeman explained that he was a former professional on the paintball circuit. His sponsor dropped him over a little *misunderstanding,* go figure. He'd then earned a degree in criminal justice and landed a job as a parking enforcement officer in Flint, Michigan. Over the next several years, he'd worked his way up to patrolman but couldn't break into the detective ranks until taking the job in Apostle Bay.

"There's a lot more action in Flint. But too many people were in line ahead of me," Freeman said. "I'd be on Social Security before I'd make detective there. That's why I came up here. Though this is not what I'd call detective work: Baby-sitting you two. If you ask me, Weathers doesn't have his head screwed on right."

I slouched further into the seat, thought about asking how the cleanup job was going in his detective's sedan, but restrained myself and watched the hotel. Demott shifted and the garbage bag covering her video camera crinkled against her yellow slicker.

Through the Jeep's windshield, I watched the hotel's main entrance. A runoff stream coursed through the parking lot, glistening in the orange sodium lights. To the right of the main entrance was a glass wall. Condensation covered the windows, hiding a view of the hotel pool. To the left, four rooms faced the parking lot. The Jeep was close enough for a good view of the rooms despite the rain.

Bits of gold light, along with an occasional blue flash of television, leaked through gaps in the curtains of the first and third rooms. Freeman said the gang boys were in room three. They'd kept the adjacent rooms empty, he said.

Greenleaf was somewhere in the hotel. A couple of sheriff's deputies were helping out, posing as a room-service waiter and a guest.

From time to time a curtain in the third room swung back and a head peeked out. I didn't see the big hair and decided it was Ketchup Boy. Freeman wouldn't let me borrow the binoculars to confirm this. He kept mumbling something that sounded like "You punks are going down," and I was hoping he wasn't referring to Lucy and me.

A light went on in room two.

"That's probably Greenleaf," Freeman said.

I leaned forward and noticed Demott did the same. Ketchup Boy peeked out. He turned, probably talking to Big Hair, and dropped the curtain.

Someone opened the curtain in room two.

I recognized something about the person in the window, but couldn't place it. He was tall, apparently a man, and he stood with his hands in his pockets and his head hanging.

A woman approached the window—I knew it was a woman because I saw the silhouette of her skirt. I watched her touch the man's shoulder. Shadows hid their faces, but I had a bad feeling in my gut.

"What the—" Freeman said. "No one's supposed to be in there."

I reached forward and yanked Freeman's binoculars from his eyes. Freeman, surprised, let them slip.

"Hey. Give those back."

I leaned out of his reach and looked through the lenses. Then I dropped the binoculars and bolted from the car.

I was halfway to the entrance before Freeman shouted "Get back here," which I had no intention of doing. Instead, I slammed through the lobby doors, almost losing it on the polished stone floor, and collided with Ken Romano, knocking him off his crutches. I dodged a family walking to the pool and turned toward the rooms. A woman moved to intercept me and I recognized her as a deputy.

"It's my wife," I said.

I feinted left and bulled past her to the second room. I tried the handle before pounding on the door.

"Deb. Open up. Open up, for God's sake."

Two claps rang out in quick succession. Then a freight train hit my back, knocking me several yards down the hall, past the drug room.

I landed face down, and my nose mashed into the burgundy-and-gold carpet. Someone wrenched my arm up and hissed, "Stay down, you fool."

The woman deputy was much heavier than she appeared.

As she crushed me to the floor, I sensed another body behind us and heard a door keyed. Glass shattered. Someone was screaming.

Someone kicked open the drug-room door and yelled, "Police!"

Another door opened and I heard Deb's voice. "Vince?"

The woman cop pushed off me and shouted, "Don't move!"

I rolled over and saw her grab Deb, yank her from the room and shove her down the hall, where Archie Freeman stood, gun drawn. Lucy Demott stood behind Freeman, filming the scene. The screaming grew louder.

Deb yelled, "What's going on?"

"Get her out of here," the woman cop yelled to Freeman, and then she turned and grabbed Tony Wittmer from the room and shoved him down the hall, too.

I sat up and looked around the corner into the drug

room. Ketchup Boy lay on the floor in a fetal position, clutching his foot and shrieking. Wind billowed the curtain behind him.

Gordon Greenleaf stood between the boy and the window, his pistol drawn.

"Uh-huh," Greenleaf grunted. "Mr. Cooperation."

THIRTY-SEVEN

"I STILL CAN'T believe you."

These were the first words Deb said to me, and she said them the moment I walked through our front door, before the lights were on, before our coats were off.

She hadn't spoken to me at the police station. Greenleaf and Chief Weathers only growled questions at me and acted like I was the criminal while Freeman kept walking by the door, muttering "Idiot" under his breath. I wasn't sure if he was talking about me or himself.

I learned from the chief that all the noise I'd made inside the Ramada had startled Homer Clump, seventeen, aka Ketchup Boy, as he was practicing his Wyatt Earp gun-twirling routine. Clump squeezed two rounds into his foot. His partner, sixteen-year-old Richie Rotel, seeing his buddy's blood and hearing the door rattle, threw a chair into the window and escaped into the parking lot. Rotel would have been snagged—more likely shot—by Archie Freeman had the rookie detective not been chasing me into the building.

Rotel was now wandering Apostle Bay and vicinity on foot.

No drugs changed hands. The cops were no closer to the seller, and Clump wasn't talking about anything except how Rotel had bailed on him. And he probably didn't have a clue who they were meeting since Rotel was ostensibly in charge.

Turns out that wet paint and fumes in the high-school library, the usual meeting spot for school-board business, had sent Deb, Tony, Ken Romano and the other negotiators to the Ramada's conference room. Another school-board member, who owns the Ramada, made the room available, the chief explained.

The Ramada staff were told to accommodate the teachers and board members "no matter what" and they did just that when the teacher committee wanted to split off for a private caucus. The desk manager gave them a key to the empty room adjacent to Ketchup Boy and Big Hair.

"I've never been so embarrassed in my life," Deb said.

"Wait until tomorrow's television news," I said.

"That's not funny."

"You're right. It's not. What I want to know is why it's such a terrible thing that I was worried about you? Anything could have happened. That bullet could have gone through the wall."

"How noble. But I can't shake the feeling that it wasn't my life you were worried about. That you'd seen me in the room with Tony, jumped to another stupid conclusion and then, once again, reacted like a buffoon."

"Now I'm a buffoon?"

I turned, walked back out the door, around the corner of our home and started toward the lake. A fog shroud concealed the water. I heard small waves washing onto the shore. The rain had stopped, but the air clung to me like wet clothes and I shivered.

She was right. Not completely. On some level I did want to get her out of there. Clump had scared me at the Big Boy more than I'd like to admit. But I was furious when I ran into that hotel, too—and jealous.

Tomorrow we'll wish we were still living in Grand Rapids, I thought. No, not tomorrow—I wish it now.

THIRTY-EIGHT

"YOU'RE SUPPOSED TO REPORT news, Vince, not make it."

Despite an overwhelming desire to duck my head and crawl under my desk, I forced my eyes to meet Lou's. I knew everyone was watching this public tongue-lashing with a mixed sense of discomfort and curiosity—at least, that's the way I'd be watching, and I wanted to show some sense of dignity, though I felt none.

"You have a good story," I whined. "We'll sell extra papers today."

"I don't know why. There's no art, not a single photo."

"C'mon, Lou. I was face down with a cop's forearm in my back."

"That is precisely the problem."

"But, Deb—"

"Shoot, Dale Weathers told me your heroics might have killed someone. Deb can take care of herself."

"What if it'd been your wife, Lou?"

"I wouldn't have been in that situation," Lou said. He paused, reached for his foam cup, looked at the contents and put it back on his desk. "Look, the bottom line is, you blew it."

"Gee, thanks."

"Get used to it. You're going to look even more foolish when the prosecutor frees Homer Clump because of your antics."

"No way he'd do that. There's got to be a weapons charge at least."

"He's doing it as we speak. Says he's trying to prevent a lawsuit against the county. If you hadn't interrupted their efforts, Clump wouldn't have been shot."

"But he shot himself. We've got to—"

"We"—he said, raising his voice to cut me off—"aren't doing anything, because you're taking some time off. Mort will cover it from here."

"C'mon, Lou. I can handle this."

Kendricks shook his head, a gesture showing both that he meant no and that he couldn't believe what an idiot I'd been.

"Things have been a little crazy for you this week, Vince. Take a few days off. Play golf. Go fishing. Drink herbal tea or something to soothe your nerves. Get away from the job. Spend time with Deb. You need it. From what I hear, you both need it."

"I'm fine. I don't need any time off."

"It's not a suggestion, Vince. I don't want to see you back here again this week."

THIRTY-NINE

I KNEW I SHOULD GO straight home from the *Chronicle* to patch things up with Deb. Instead I walked five blocks south to the Superior County Courthouse and was now sitting in the document room trying to find the deed to a tavern once known as the Lost Moose.

The document room was a study in brown, from the paneling to the leather-bound map books. The darkness sucked what little light the brass desk lamps shed, as if trying to protect the timeworn documents from further decay.

I liked the room. On a normal day there was something exhilarating about digging through the old records, reading formal language, studying handwritten transactions and wondering what the writer had been like.

This time the phone book had proved fruitless in my search, but I'd hit pay dirt with another call to Patrice. She'd connected me with a local history buff, the proprietor of an antiques shop west of town.

"The place is the Iron Inn now," the guy had told me. "But it was once the Lost Moose. I saw the old sign in the basement when I appraised some old bar equipment."

The history buff didn't know the original owner.

I started with the Iron Inn liquor license. This gave

me particulars to pull property records. From there I found Charles Stinson. Stinson had built the Lost Moose fifty-three years ago. He sold the tavern a dozen years back.

A search for other property owned by Stinson turned up a forty-acre tract, fifteen miles northwest of Apostle Bay. A hunting camp, I guessed. Most folks in Northern Michigan had a "forty" for hunting. They paid the taxes by select-logging the land every five-to-seven years, taking the largest trees and clearing the way for smaller ones to grow.

I found two Stinsons in the directory—neither of them named Charles. The second was a cousin, and she said Charles had moved to Pensacola, Florida, after selling the tavern. He returned every November for the firearm deer season, but that was the extent of his time in Michigan.

Sitting on the courthouse steps, using that day's edition of the *Chronicle* to insulate my rear against the cold granite, I called the man.

"Your name is Marshall, eh? I knew a doc up there named Marshall. Any relation?"

My old man must have treated everybody.

"He was my dad. This is somewhat related to him. I'm looking for information about an employee of yours. It would have been about thirty years ago."

"Doubt I can help you, son. I have trouble remembering what day it is. I tell time by what pill I'm popping. I can't remember half the people who worked for me, and for that matter, I don't want to. There were some good ones, but most of them were bums who would rob the till if I turned my back a second."

"This employee was a young Native American woman. She married a rich kid from Elk Ridge."

"William Pontcliff," Stinson said immediately. "Yeah, her name was Autumn Coyote. Darn shame about those two. What's your interest?"

I needed a moment to remember Pontcliff was Vanessa Grey's married name.

"Sounds like your memory isn't so bad," I said.

"Some people are hard to forget. Again, what's your interest?"

"It's a long story, really. The short version is that Autumn's sister, a woman named April, died this week. April was searching for information about her sister and she didn't have much to go on. I've kind of, well…I've taken up her search."

"Why?"

"As I mentioned, this also has to do with my dad. April Coyote believed my dad caused her sister's death. Someone put that thought in her mind. I'm trying to find out what really happened."

"Well, son, I can tell you your dad didn't kill that girl. A snowstorm and a couple tons of pickup truck did."

"Really?"

"I remember her well. I'd guess you could say my wife and I kind of adopted Autumn and William. We tried to help them. She waited tables for me and was a sharp gal. She remembered orders without writing them down, though it's not like we had an extensive menu.

Most people ordered onion rings and pitchers of Stroh's. William was my dishwasher. He was hopeless. Broke more dishes than he washed. But I give him credit. He tried to do the right thing.

"They lived in my hunting camp, in an old trailer I have on a forty northwest of town. I'd lent them the place until they could afford something of their own. I still have that trailer, out behind my cabin now. There are trees growing right up through the floor and out the roof, but it's still there." Stinson paused and I sensed I shouldn't interrupt.

"My wife and I were heartbroken when they died."

"You know who William Grey, uh, Pontcliff was?"

"Sure I do. Ironic, isn't it?"

"What's that?"

"You know, him cleaning the dishes of the men he owned. His family owned them anyway—paid their wages. It was mostly miners who spent money in my tavern. I paid him with that money. Funny how things go in a circle."

"So it's true he split from his family?"

"His old lady tossed him out when he married Autumn. She was a beauty and, like I said, smart, too. She was pregnant, you know. They were good kids. It's sad what happened to them."

"What did happen?"

"The newspaper said it was a head-on collision, slippery roads. Everyone died. There weren't many details, as I recall. I always thought it strange that it happened in the middle of the night and during a snowstorm. Don't know why they were out that late. They'd both been working that evening. I tried talking to the cops to find out, but they wouldn't give me the time of day. Kind of think his family had something to do with that."

"What about the baby?"

"Like I said, I couldn't get any more information. But from what I heard, nobody survived."

FORTY

WHEN MONTY HAVER could breathe again—hauling his three-hundred-pound bulk up the fifty-two courthouse steps had been a prodigious effort—he spoke the words I was now sick of hearing: "Hey, buddy, saw you on the news this morning."

"That was my evil twin."

"Are you moonlighting as the hotel's carpet inspector?" Haver asked. "Actually, you didn't look too bad. Did you catch Ken Romano? He looked like a deer caught in someone's headlights."

"Romano? No. I didn't watch the news."

"Good thing. It wasn't pretty. You have a moment? Come on in and tell me about it. I'd like a first-hand account."

"Sure," I said. I liked Monty Haver, and I owed the guy. Haver, in his fourth term as the Superior County clerk, knew just about everything when it came to court filings, births, deaths, marriages, divorces and all-around gossip. He was a fifth-generation Apostle Bay resident.

We went through the heavy entrance doors, doors as ponderous as Haver himself, and walked toward the clerk's office. To get there we passed through a rotunda lined with portraits of all the circuit court judges who had served Superior County for the last century and a half, then turned down a stone corridor and walked on a floor worn smooth by scuffing feet and cheapened with removable rubber mats. The big man moved slowly and kept wiping sweat from his forehead and neck.

"Monty, if you don't mind my asking, why did you walk up those stairs? You have a reserved parking place on the back side of the building. You can walk up three steps to your office. You tackle those front stairs much more and your heart's going to burst."

"Doc's orders. Well, really it's for my grandkids. The doctor has been telling me for years to get exercise, eat rabbit food and drop some of this weight. I said forget that. But I'm starting to think I'd like to be around to see those two munchkins grow up. So I'm going to give his plan a try."

He stopped and fished his wallet out. Inside were two photos, an infant in a purple-and-gold Minnesota Vikings sleeper, and a girl toddler in a Vikings cheerleader costume.

"That's a noble cause," I said. "But maybe you should start with something less strenuous."

"I take it one step at a time." He smiled and returned his wallet to his back pocket.

A SMALLER MAN would have looked silly behind Monty Haver's gargantuan wood desk, but Haver did the desk and expansive office justice. Like the document room, the office was a study in wood, stained tea-brown and polished to a sheen. The desk matched the oak wain-scoting surrounding the room. If not for the three tall and narrow east-facing windows that ran from waist to ceiling, the office would have been oppressively dark.

On election nights, when Monty held court for all the media and announced incoming results, he'd keep the lights low, like he was hosting a séance. Haver said he was respecting the building's history. I thought Haver was a born showman and that he enjoyed making the entire process seem mysterious.

Deputy Clerk Rhonda Wentworth—blonde and pale as a naked mole rat, looking schoolmarmish in her cardigan sweater and long, wool skirt—joined us. She started a new pot of coffee brewing and sat on the edge of Haver's desk, while Haver lowered himself into his chair. I sat on the visitor side and gave them an edited version of the previous night's events.

"I bet you feel like a horse's patootie," Wentworth said after I had finished.

"Give the man a break, Rhonda. He was rescuing his wife."

"If I'm ever in trouble, I hope my knight in shining armor doesn't end up tripping over his feet and lying on the floor," Wentworth said. Then she smiled, hopped off the desk and lightly touched the rug burn on my cheek. "You know I'm just kidding you, Vince. You like your coffee straight-up, right?"

I nodded. While Rhonda poured, Haver poked fun at the other locals caught on the news video. He mentioned

Ken Romano again, and Rhonda laughed at another rendition of Romano's surprised look.

An idea struck me as I watched Haver's mimicry.

"Speaking of Romano, he hasn't turned up in any court cases recently, has he?" I asked.

Haver leaned back. He sipped his coffee, then said, "I recognize that tone, boy. Your mind's working a story. What do you have?"

"Just wondering. Anyone suing him?"

I noticed Rhonda look at Haver, nod, then move off the desk. She left the room.

"Not exactly," Haver said.

"What's that supposed to mean?"

"You going to tell me why you're asking?"

"Does it matter?"

"You know it does, Vince."

Rhonda reentered and placed two folders on Haver's desk. Both she and Haver looked at me. I knew without a doubt the folders had some dirt on Ken Romano. I also knew Haver would bury them somehow if he wanted to. I was sure the man had protected people that way in the past, through lost or *misplaced* files, but couldn't prove it and couldn't do a thing about it.

"It's just a fishing expedition, Monty. I really don't have anything but a gut feeling."

"If you're looking to smear Ken Romano, I won't help."

I looked at them both, then glanced at the files again. I told them about Greenleaf's theory.

"No way," Wentworth said. "You really think?"

"Like I said, I'm just on a fishing expedition. I'll bet Gordon will ask the same thing soon. If he hasn't already."

"Probably hasn't because you gave him something else to worry about," Haver said. He smiled and pushed the folders toward me. "Our standard deal applies."

The standard deal: I didn't tell anyone about the clerk's help, and I told Haver and Wentworth about the story before it ran in the newspaper so they could win brownie points in gossip circles. I nodded and took the files.

Both manila folders were lawsuits against a company called KRI, a second-tier subsidiary of Romano Auto Sales. The first was by an out-of-state contractor who hadn't been paid for building a new auto showroom. He was suing KRI for about half a million. The other was by four employees claiming their employer, KRI, hadn't paid their medical-insurance premiums. All four had been denied treatment because of the overdue premium.

Son-of-a-gun, I thought. This should help patch things up with Gordon.

FORTY-ONE

"BACK AGAIN SO soon?"

Patrice Berklee climbed from the vault like a raven on the rise to answer my bell ring. I wondered if she ever wore clothes that weren't black. Even her cotton gloves were black today, stained by old newsprint.

"Any luck on your search?" Her voice was friendlier than I'd heard on any previous trip.

"You bet," I said. "The woman who jumped off Eagle's Cliff? Well, her younger sister was an employee at Elk Ridge, and it turns out she married William Pont-cliff and was pregnant with his child."

"That's interesting," Patrice said. She pulled off her gloves and sat, waving me to the chair opposite her desk. She opened a journal and jotted a note. "I wonder how they got family approval."

"They didn't. The story is that Vanessa Grey tried to prevent the marriage, and when she couldn't, she kicked her son out.

"I may have tracked them further thanks to your antiques-shop friend," I added. "But I need your help again." I explained what Charles Stinson told me.

"Let's browse back issues of the *Chronicle* for an accident report," Patrice said. "Is there any way to narrow the search?"

"Stinson told me the accident was the first big snow-storm of the season. And it was before hunting season. That would make it any time between mid-October to early November."

Patrice stepped back into the vault. "I'll pick up rolls from twenty-eight to thirty-two years ago." Her voice faded as she climbed down the ladder. "We'll spin those and see what turns up."

I settled into a microfiche carrel, leaned back and stretched. This was going to take time, I thought.

PATRICE FOUND THE STORY on her third roll. The date was October 28, thirty-two years ago.

STEEL HEIR DEAD IN AUTO ACCIDENT
SEASON'S FIRST STORM KILLS THREE

Apostle Bay—William Peter Grey Pontcliff, 20, heir to the Grey Industries steel fortune, was tragi-cally killed this morning in an accident when two pickup trucks collided on State Highway 28, 10 miles west of Apostle Bay.

Also killed were 59-year-old John "Spike" Anderson of Whitetail Junction and Autumn Coyote, 17. Anderson operated heavy equipment at the Huron Range Eastern Pit. Coyote was re-portedly a former employee of the exclusive Elk Ridge Hunt and Fish Club.

William Pontcliff was the son of Rochester and Vanessa Pontcliff, majority shareholders of Grey Industries, a multimillion-dollar conglomerate that owns and operates all the iron mines on the Huron Range, as well as steel mills throughout the Midwest. The company is this region's leading employer.

Pontcliff was a resident of Chicago but a frequent visitor at Elk Ridge, a private enclave that the Grey family founded. Club members and company officials refused to speak with the Chronicle *regarding the accident.*

Coyote was a passenger in the truck driven by Pontcliff, said patrolman Dale Weathers of the Apostle Bay police. All three victims died at the crash site.

"It was a bloody mess," said Waino Toivola, the first person on the scene. "Those two trucks were crunched like accordions. The bodies were tossed out like rag dolls. Worst thing I've ever seen except that time Rolf Mathiason fell in the quarry's rock crusher a few years back."

The crash occurred during this season's first winter blizzard. Slippery roads, as well as poor visibility, likely contributed to the accident, Weathers said.

St. Mark's Hospital Ambulance Service also responded to the scene.

Additional information regarding the accident was not available at press time.

Patrice also found a lengthy obituary for John "Spike" Anderson in the following day's edition. We could not find any follow-up stories on the accident, nor an obituary or death notice for Coyote or Pontcliff.

I dropped into the chair next to Patrice. "It seems odd to me that's the only story considering the social status of Pontcliff."

"Maybe the family had more influence over the newspaper than you'd like to believe," Patrice said. "I see it in history all the time. Notice the story doesn't say anything about Autumn Coyote being pregnant, if indeed she was, or that she and Pontcliff were married, if they really were. If we spent a little more time at this, we might discover that Grey Industries increased their advertising in the paper during the next few months or made a donation to the publisher's favorite charity. You'd be surprised, Vince. If you want more depth, you have to read between the lines, you have to keep digging, and you have to wonder about the information that's missing."

"Okay, but where would I go from here?"

"Why don't you try asking *patrolman* Dale Weathers what he remembers?"

"There's a minor problem with that. He's not talking to me right now."

My cell phone chirped. I looked at the caller ID, then my watch. "Oh, man, I'm in trouble now."

FORTY-TWO

"Hi, Deb."

"Where are you? I'm looking like a fool here in the Kiddie Academy waiting room. I called the paper. They said you're off today."

"I'm five minutes away," I said.

We'd scheduled a site visit to the daycare center last week and I'd forgotten.

"You're twenty minutes late. Forget it. I'll do the tour without you. When you want to join our life again, let me know."

"That's not fair."

"It's more than fair considering what you told your mother."

"What are you—"

I was speaking to dead air.

"Gotta run," I told Patrice.

I jogged out the door. Once inside my Bronco I swung out of the alley and onto Apostle Bay's main street, ignored a driver leaning on her horn and cut up through a different alley behind the movie theater. Practicing all my reporter-racing-to-the-scene skills, I was able to make the five-minute estimate.

Inside the Kiddie Academy, I was guided to a large

red, blue and green playroom, where Deb was meeting with the daycare center's owner. Deb glared. I thought the owner flashed me a dirty look, too, but she held out her hand and turned on the salesperson's charm when I approached. Glory was beyond the two women, digging in a plastic toy bin and tossing stuffed animals out onto the floor.

"Hi, sorry I'm late," I said.

Glory looked up toward my voice. Then she threw down the toys she held, kicked her legs and let out a wail.

I approached and crouched to her level. "Hey, Glory—"

She cut me off with a stiff-arm to my Adam's apple.

Deb stepped between us and lifted Glory. "Daddy came to see your special place with us."

"All the animals wondered where you went," the owner said. She lifted Glory from Deb's arms. "Let's go back and tell them you can stay and play." She turned to Deb and me and told us to explore the place, including the outdoor play yard and library, while she occupied our daughter.

Deb pulled me away.

"Nice entrance," she said.

"I'm sorry I'm late."

"You're not sorry," she hissed. "You're embarrassed. There's a difference."

"Truce. I'm here now. Let's tour this place. When we finish, let's grab a bite of fast food. Maybe we can talk things out while Glory crawls around in the play land,"

"There is no way I'm going into a restaurant in this

town after our TV debut this morning. It's bad enough being here. And the *Chronicle*'s story made things worse. According to that jerk Mort Maki, the teachers' bargaining committee was dealing drugs, not those punks."

"Deb, we have to—"

"You're right," she interrupted. "We need to talk. But not here."

FORTY-THREE

"What did my mother tell you?"

Half-eaten burgers and fries littered our kitchen table. Drive-thru fast food had sounded good at the daycare center, but neither Deb nor I had much of an appetite now.

Deb leaned against the kitchen doorjamb. A *Veggie Tales* video echoed behind her, and she hummed the song. I guessed a tomato was now singing to our daughter.

I looked away from Deb and busied my hands with the day's mail: A few bills, two catalogs and a hand-addressed letter to me. The handwriting seemed familiar, but there was no return address. I pushed the mail away, knowing I'd better give Deb my full attention.

"She told me that you think I'm having an affair," Deb said.

I glanced up and saw her eyes were moist.

"I, uh—"

"How could you say that?" she asked. "I knew you were being stupid about Tony, but I didn't realize it had gone this far. And to tell your mother but not talk to me?"

I stood and stepped in her direction.

"No," she said, raising her palm to warn me back. "It

makes sense now. All this started after Glory's birth. You started working crazy hours, staying away from home, acting moody. I don't think you've been happy since she was born."

"C'mon, Deb. I love Glory."

"Those are just words. You find excuses to work and to drop her off at your mom's house. Oh, you go through the motions. You change her diapers and put her to bed. But you act so pathetic that I end up doing it most of the time." She was still whispering. "It's too late to decide you don't want a child. You're in this for the long haul."

"It's not that, Deb. It's just…you can't blame me for being jealous, for wondering about Tony. He followed you up here from Grand Rapids. He's around you a lot."

"He followed me up here because he needed a job. And he's an excellent teacher. He's around a lot because we're friends. We're also trying to negotiate a new contract, and it's like beating our heads on a brick wall and I can't share that frustration with you because of your newspaper job, so I have to share it with him."

"It's more than that, Deb. He knows Glory better than I do. He puts her to bed better than I do."

"That's because he spends more time with her."

"And why is that?"

"Yeah, why is that?"

That hurt, because I knew she had a point. Instead of conceding, I looked away.

"Did you ever think that maybe I encourage him because I need a break?" Deb said. "Because I can't survive on baby babble by myself? Because sometimes if I have to read one more Dr. Seuss book I'll puke? He gives me a break because you don't."

"You encourage it?"

"Of course. And don't get on your high horse and act jealous. If anyone should be jealous, it's your daughter and me. We can't compete with your job."

"You're exaggerating, Deb. I'm not gone that much of the time."

Deb snorted and threw her arms in the air. "No. You're gone all day and half the nights. You listen to the scanner on the weekends and run out on a moment's notice. All your energy is reserved for your job."

"That's—"

"Why can't you look at the bigger picture? Whatever you write today is forgotten tomorrow, or the next day or the next week. We're real: Glory and me. Not April Coyote. Not some Elk Ridge widow who insists people call her by some stupid royal title. We are the story that you're neglecting. And we won't go on this way forever."

FORTY-FOUR

GLORY CHRISTENED the next morning with milk and Cheerios. Then she taught me a new meaning for the expression "bad hair day."

It all started when I stepped away from her highchair to brew coffee. As I poured water into the pot, I heard a similar splashing sound behind me. After a moment's consideration, I whirled to see Glory dumping the final white drops onto the floor.

I returned my daughter's delighted grin, grabbed paper towels and stooped to clean the mess. Under Glory's chair, while I corralled Cheerios, something soft touched my head. I reached up, expecting to find Glory's hand, and came away with a wad of mashed banana.

"Glory!"

Deep breaths, I told myself. Take deep breaths.

"That is not funny."

But it must have been because Glory giggled. She kept giggling as I wiped her face, pulled her from the highchair and sent her to the other room. On her way she grabbed a stack of papers from the table, spilling some into the milk, carrying others with her. She looked back, daring me to chase her, and then ran. I let her go.

I'd retrieve the unopened bills and stuff after I finished cleaning the breakfast mess.

I wiped the milk and cereal, tried to pick some banana from my hair and then poured a mug of coffee.

"Glory, you need to give me those papers now," I said. I walked into the living room and—

"You little…"

Black vermiculite-flecked potting soil covered the floor and couch. Every houseplant lay on its side in overturned terra cotta pots. Dirt clods trailed past the television to Glory's room.

In her room, I found Glory feeding the soil to her stuffed animals. I returned to the kitchen, grabbed the phone and called Mom. Too bad answering machines can't dispense motherly advice.

By HALF PAST ONE, when Gordon Greenleaf called my cell phone, I still wore sweatpants, T-shirt and a banana 'do. Glory and the house were equally messy. I was ready for adult conversation.

"Vince, I have bad news."

"There's nothing you can tell me that's worse than this morning, Gordon."

"How about you need to get down here now? We arrested Deb an hour ago."

"Right, Gordo. That's a good—"

"I'm not joking. For possession of narcotics."

A crash echoed from the kitchen. I strode through the door and found Glory emptying the dirty dishes from the dishwasher onto the floor.

"You probably want to contact a lawyer before you come," Greenleaf said.

"What are you talking about, Gordon?"

"We found our marijuana source. Tony Wittmer's trunk was half full of pot. That's all I can say. As a friend I'm telling you to get Deb a lawyer and get down here."

"I can't believe this," I said, crumpling to the floor.

GLORY TUGGED MY SLEEVE. She was silent for once, and her eyes showed fear. Funny how kids figure things out.

"C'mon, Glory, Mommy needs our help."

I pulled her against my chest and looked over her shoulder at my cell phone. I dialed Mom's number; still no answer, so I left a message. Then I stood, dug a phone book from the kitchen drawer and searched for attorneys, stopping at someone who'd impressed me during a court case I'd covered for the newspaper: Sarah Dodge. Should have thought of her first. I called, gave a short explanation to her secretary, then asked for a call back.

I wrapped Glory in her coat, skipping shoes. They didn't fit over her sleeper feet.

"Okay, Morning Glory, let's go find out what's happening."

CHAOS RULED the police-station lobby. I caught sight of Lucy Demott and Mort Maki waiting outside the dispatch center. A few of Deb's friends I recognized from teacher functions and some teens, probably students, were talking with them. There was also the usual hodgepodge of people arriving to dispute parking tickets, but now sticking around to see if they could get on TV.

I made a U-turn when I saw the crowd and walked around to the employee entrance behind city hall. An empty patrol car idled by an unmarked door.

"Let's see if we can get in a different way, kiddo."

I shifted Glory, pulled the phone from my pocket and called the police number. Gail Stevens answered.

"Hi, Gail. It's, Vince."

"Oh. Um…how are you doing?"

"Swell, as you can imagine. Can you please have someone let me in the rear entrance? I'm here with my daughter, and I don't want to drag her through that crowd out by your desk."

"Just a second."

I smiled at the security camera. Moments later Gordon Greenleaf swung the door open. He gave me an odd look, started to say something, then stopped and waved us through. He patted Glory's arm when I passed.

"Deb is in my office. We're letting her go home with you. We think she was just in the wrong place at the wrong time."

Greenleaf started down the hall, but I grabbed his arm and pulled him back.

"Give me details before I see her."

"I can't, buddy. The chief is at Clark's office now. They'll decide what information to release."

"Gordon, this is Deb we're talking about here. I'm not a reporter now. I'm her husband."

Greenleaf hesitated, then nodded at Glory. She was

calm in my arms, as if she sensed this wasn't the time to act up.

"It's okay, Gordon."

"We pulled Tony Wittmer over for a traffic stop about half past noon. When we searched his trunk, we found the dope. Like I said on the phone, his trunk was half full of—"

"What do you mean, searched his trunk? For a traffic stop?"

Greenleaf stayed silent.

"You had a tip, didn't you?"

"He's the guy, Vince. I did a little digging after the arrest. Do you know he left his previous school under bad circumstances? I don't have the details yet, but he was basically forced to resign."

"Are you serious? Deb helped him get the job here. I can't believe she'd do that if what you're saying is true."

"Even the best are fooled. She's waiting for you."

Greenleaf turned and walked down the corridor. I followed, my sneakers squeaking on the polished vinyl floor. We passed by a few offices. I heard cops talking but didn't look into the rooms. Instead I kept my eyes on Greenleaf's back and nuzzled my face against Glory's hair.

"Everything's going to be okay, kiddo," I whispered.

DEB LEAPED from the plastic seat—the same one I usually sat in for morning coffee. She wrapped her arms around us. Tears streaked her face and I felt them against my cheek. Glory reached for Deb and I handed her over.

"I'm going to give you guys a few minutes alone," Greenleaf said. "We'll release you soon, Deb. When we do, you can go out the back again."

Greenleaf left the office and closed the door.

"I guess you're getting your fifteen minutes of fame all in one week," I said.

Deb stepped back and wiped her eyes with a tissue.

"You guys are a mess," she said. "Were you digging out in the yard in your pajamas? What's that in your hair?"

"It's a long story. Tell me what happened."

"We were set up. There's no other answer."

"C'mon, Deb. I know you're hurt, but Gordon says it's a clean bust. He's a good detective. Tony's the guy they've been looking for all summer. It makes sense. He has access to the kids."

"Vince, get real."

"Then tell me what happened."

She sat in the chair with Glory on her lap and brushed dirt from our daughter's sleeper. I leaned against the door.

"A bunch of teachers ordered takeout from the diner. Tony volunteered to pick it up. I rode with him. A police car pulled in behind us when we left the school parking lot. They followed us to the diner and were still waiting outside when we came out with the order. We both thought it was strange. Then they followed us back to the school. About a block away, they flashed their lights and Tony pulled over. The cop who came to the window said Tony was going slightly over the speed limit. Then he asked Tony to open his trunk. Tony said "Sure" and popped the release. The next thing I know, another patrol car pulls in front of us—lights flashing. They order us out of the car and push me against the back door. A cop I couldn't even see read me my rights, pinched my wrists in cuffs and dragged me into the first patrol car. They took Tony away in the other car and I haven't seen him since. It was humiliating."

"Worse than the other night?" I said, attempting a smile.

"Yeah, a lot worse." She snuggled Glory again and said, "I'm glad you're not old enough to watch the news."

"Gordon said you were in the wrong place at the wrong time. I'm sorry. I called Sarah Dodge to represent you. She's the best lawyer in this town."

"We're going to need one when Tony and I sue the pants off whoever did this to us."

"Tony and you?" I turned my face toward the door and banged my head against it. "Why are you defending this guy? Look what he's done to you. I've been saying he's bad news and I was right. Can't I be right for once?"

I spun around and saw she was standing.

"How stupid do you think I am, Vince? Too stupid to know if my friend is dealing drugs to teens? Tony's not a drug dealer."

"Better people than you have been fooled."

"C'mon, Vince, think about it. If your trunk was loaded with pot, would you agree to pop it open in broad daylight, without a fuss, because some cop pulled you over for supposedly going a few miles over the speed limit?"

There was a soft knock. I stepped away from the door and let Greenleaf in.

"The chief called. You can leave, for now."

He handed Deb her coat and purse.

"What does 'for now' mean?" I asked.

"Deb's not being charged—at this time."

"Tell the chief he can talk to her lawyer next time."

Greenleaf nodded. "Let's get you out of here before Clark changes his mind."

I lifted Glory from Deb and she put her coat on. We retraced the path to the rear entrance. Greenleaf stopped before opening the door and pulled me aside.

"Listen, buddy, Clark's out for blood on this one. Deb needs to play it smart."

I nodded and turned to leave.

"There's something else, on a different subject," Greenleaf said. "Elk Ridge security called us yesterday. I thought you might like to know this. A woman named Helen Verba is missing. She was—"

"Vanessa Grey's nurse. I know."

"Something's up. They wanted our help finding her. She's been missing since the night the old lady died."

"Do they think she had something to do with the death?"

"They didn't say. The sheriff's got Search and Rescue up there combing the woods for her now."

"Thanks for letting me know." I started toward the door again.

"One other thing," Greenleaf said. "I asked about the

chief's visit while I had them on the phone. They told me it was a short one. He and your mother didn't get in."

"What do you mean, he and my mother?"

"She was with him. They tried to see the old lady, but security turned them away. That was it. At least, that's what the guards told me."

"Thanks, Gord. And thanks for helping Deb. Sorry I was being a jerk back there."

FORTY-FIVE

SARAH DODGE CALLED my cell phone as we stepped outside.

"I'm at the courthouse, just left a hearing," she said. I recognized her confident voice. That's what I remembered most about seeing her in court—she acted like she was in charge.

"Are you at the police station?" she asked.

"We're leaving now. They're letting Deb go."

"Good. Where can we meet?"

"Let me put Deb on. She can tell you what happened."

We walked around the building corner as I handed her the phone.

"It's Sarah Dodge, the attorney I told you about."

Deb took the phone. I looked ahead toward the parking lot and saw Mort Maki peeking in my Bronco's windows. I stopped Deb, pulled her back around the corner.

"I'll get the car," I said. "Wait for me here."

Deb put her hand over the phone and mouthed "Why?"

"You've had enough publicity for one week."

Before she could argue, I readjusted Glory on my hip and walked quietly until I was behind Maki.

"Find anything interesting?" I said.

Maki jumped. "I thought this was your car. Where's your wife?"

I opened the rear passenger door, climbed in and settled Glory into her car seat. Maki held the door open, invading my personal space while I strapped her in.

"C'mon. What can you tell me, buddy?" he asked.

"They're going to move Wittmer over to the courthouse for a preliminary hearing. Soon. Your best chance for a photo is when they come through the front door."

"How soon?" Maki asked, letting go of the door and looking toward the building.

I pushed him away, yanked the door closed and hit the lock. Then I climbed over and into the driver's seat, while he pounded the glass. I started the engine and pulled away.

At the back entrance, Deb climbed in.

"What did Sarah say?"

"I'm going to meet her in two hours at her office. She's going to the police station first to take care of Tony."

"What the—? I hired her for you."

"I don't need a lawyer, okay? I didn't do anything wrong. Besides, I'm on my way home. He's the one in jail."

"Then let him get his own lawyer. What is it with you and this guy?"

"I'm telling you this was a setup."

From the corner of my eye, I watched as she rubbed her temples.

"Now I know what those kids must have felt like," she said.

"Setup or not, Deb, it's time to watch out for yourself. Do I need to replay your words to me from last night? You won't do Glory or me any good if you go down trying to defend Tony Wittmer. This is about more than being arrested. It could cost you your job, even your teaching career."

"Drop me off at the school, Vince."

"I'm taking you home."

"To do what? My car is at the school. My friends are there, wondering what happened."

"You mean your friends are there gossiping about you."

"I need to get back to school," Deb said. She reached across and touched my arm. "I'll just get a few things and go straight to the lawyer's office. I promise."

She tipped her head toward the back. I adjusted the rearview mirror and saw Glory sleeping.

THE SCHOOL'S WEST-SIDE entrance is a pair of glass doors set in a blank two-story brick wall. I've often wondered at the architect's aversion to windows when he designed Bay High. It's a rectangular box with only eight real windows. These gave the administrative staff a chance to see daylight. Another half-dozen faux windows had been spaced along the street-side facade so parents driving by might think their child was getting natural light. Apparently the plan was to keep the outside world from distracting students.

I pulled in next to Deb's black Chevy Cavalier and checked the rearview mirror to see Glory still sleeping.

"You want me to come in?" I asked.

"No. I'll grab some stuff, be in and out in two minutes. See you at home after I meet with Sarah Dodge."

I watched her go through the glass doors, then circled the school.

On the east side I passed five cars parked as close to the entrance as possible. A half-dozen people stood outside the door, apparently waiting for someone to unlock it. One of them leaned on crutches. Seeing Romano jogged my memory.

I reached for my cell to call Gordon and tell him about the KRI files. Instead, the phone rang when I grabbed it.

"Vince, it's Patrice Berklee. How would you like to meet Waino Toivola, the guy who saw the accident?"

FORTY-SIX

TEN MINUTES LATER I pulled into the Lakeview Elder Care parking lot. I checked the mirror, combed a few curls with my fingers, then gave up. My hair was flat. It smelled like banana, and there wasn't much I could do about it now. I searched for a tissue in my coat pockets and found a paper scrap and spoonful of crumbs.

I tossed the crumbs in the grass and double-checked the scrap. It was the note Helen slipped me the night I visited Elk Ridge. The writing looked similar to…to the letter I'd looked at last night but never opened. It was in the stack of things Glory took this morning.

I shoved it back into my pocket as a reminder to find the letter when we got home, then searched through junk in my back seat until I found a crunched ball cap.

As I smoothed out the cap's worst wrinkles, my scanner belched a blast of static and it woke Glory. She took a quick glance at her surroundings and promptly started to scream. I whispered a curse and switched the thing off before unbuckling her. I tried calming her and cleaning some of the dirt off her PJs, not succeeding at either.

Glory continued crying as I carried her across the parking lot. She cried as the reception nurse shot me a wrinkled frown that said "No screaming children allowed."

"I'm here to see Waino Toivola," I said. "His son is supposed to meet me in the lobby."

I felt a tug on my sleeve and looked down into the bluest eyes and bluest hair I'd ever seen. They belonged to a small woman with skin so translucent it also had a bluish tinge. She was riding in a wheelchair.

"Here's a cookie for your little girl," she said, her voice firm, holding more strength than seemed possible for such a fragile-looking human.

Glory had stopped crying and looked at the woman, too. The lady reached into her sleeve and pulled out a fresh tissue.

"Don't just stand there. Wipe her eyes. Then give her this cookie."

I thanked the woman and wiped Glory's face and nose. I glanced at the receptionist and saw her nod before I took the cookie.

"Would you like this, Glory?"

Glory grabbed the cookie and bit off a small chunk.

"That's a funny name," the blue lady said. She wheeled away.

She rolled past a towering man who seemed as big as a virgin white pine. His smile and chipmunk cheeks pushed his eyes into tiny slits.

"Vince Marshall?" he asked. "I'm Waino's son, Rod. Glad to meetcha."

Rod Toivola clamped down on my free hand and pumped until I bobbled Glory.

"Read your stuff all the time," he said. "Your daddy delivered me, you know."

"You don't say." The sarcasm was lost on him.

"We're all excited that you want to interview Papa. Shoot, we got him duded up in his best pajamas for you. He don't wear clothes no more. Absolutely refuses to. Says as long as he's in bed he's wearin' pajamas. Guess you can't argue with that."

"I guess not."

I watched Blue Lady wheel into and out of various rooms down the corridor ahead of us.

"Now, I'll tell you, Mr. Marshall," Rod Toivola said in a conspiratorial whisper, "you got to take anything Papa says with a grain of salt, if you know what I mean. His memory ain't too good. Kinda comes and goes like the TV when the weather's blowin' the antenna around."

"Sure. Does he remember the accident?"

"Hard to tell. He doesn't hear too well, either, so what he says sometimes don't make much sense."

Blue Lady backed out of a room and pointed toward us. Then an aluminum walker rolled out of the doorway, pushed by a frail woman not more than four feet tall. They stared, giggled and moved down the corridor. I heard Glory laugh and saw she was watching the women, too.

"Well, c'mon," Rod said, bouncing on his toes with excitement. "We'd better get to Papa before his nap starts."

A THOUSAND, no, two thousand eyes stared at us when we entered Waino Toivola's room. I needed a moment for my own peepers to focus and realize all the staring eyes belonged to deer. Pictures of trophy deer cut from hunting magazines covered every vertical surface.

"Ya like it?" Rod asked. "We're a huntin' family. Breaks Papa's heart every fall when we go to camp and he can't come. So I decorated his room for him."

"What? Is this him, Roddy?" The scratchy voice of a lifelong smoker came from the hospital bed on the room's far side.

I watched an emaciated man lean forward, brush aside the tubes bringing oxygen to his nostrils and stare with huge, bulbous eyes.

"You don't look like Doc Marshall."

"He's not, Papa. This is his son."

"I know he's not his papa, you idiot. Don't look like his son, neither. What you got there in your arms? A kid? Oh, Missy Blue's going to wet her PJs."

I moved toward the bed. Glory squirmed. At first I thought she feared Waino or the multitude of eyes, then I saw she was reaching toward the door. The blue-haired lady and her friend were there, also a young nurse's aide.

"Can Glory play?" Missy Blue asked. "I have some toys in my room she might like. I keep them for my grandchildren."

The aide stepped through the door and whispered, "Her grandchildren never come. But she keeps toys in her room in case they do. Honestly, spending time with a toddler brightens her day so much. Can we borrow your daughter for a few minutes? We're just across the hall and I'll be with her."

Glory decided the issue when she writhed from my arms and toddled toward Missy Blue without fear.

"I guess it's okay," I said.

"I'll stay with her," the aide said. She reached down to take Glory's hand.

I shook my head and wondered why everyone else had such an easy time with the girl. Then I turned back to Waino. The old man waved his hand in disgust and then fell back onto the bed.

"I wanted to ask you some questions about a car accident thirty years ago," I said.

"Eh, dirty? What? Dirty sheets? Roddy, call that little nurse in here to change them."

Waino pushed himself forward as if he was going to stand.

"No, Papa," Roddy shouted and came to his father's side. "He said thirty years. A car accident." He turned to me and said, "You'll have to speak up."

"Who had an accident?" Waino shouted. "Is that why my sheets are dirty?"

Waino pushed his blanket back and yanked his pajama bottoms open. I averted my eyes, then asked, "Roddy, can he see well enough to read?"

"Sure. Nothing wrong with his eyesight since he had that cat-track surgery."

I wrote a question on my notepad while Waino inspected his crotch.

"See, I told ya I didn't have no accident, Roddy."

"Car accident!" I shouted. "A long time ago." I held the pad in front of Waino's face.

"Eh?" Waino squinted at the pad. Then he turned to Roddy. "What's that say, Roddy?"

I gave Roddy a questioning look.

"You didn't ask me if he could read," Roddy said. "Just if he could see."

Great, I thought. I took the pad back, drew a quick sketch of two cars crashing, snowflakes falling and a stick man standing by the cars. Then I added three stick figures lying on the ground by the cars, one with long hair and a dress. I held the pad under Waino's nose again. After he looked for a moment, I touched Waino's chest, then pointed to the stick figure standing by the cars.

"Can't draw worth beans, can you?" Waino said.

Then he pointed at the picture and asked if it happened a long time ago. I nodded.

"This the one that killed Spike?"

I thought a moment, remembered Spike Anderson was a victim and then nodded.

"Then it was trucks that crashed, not cars," Waino said. "It was a bloody mess. They"—and here he pointed to the cars in the picture—"were crunched like accordions."

"That's what you said in the *Chronicle,*" I answered. "Was there a baby?"

"Ain't no maybe about it. I remember it like it was yesterday on account of the kid. Doc delivered that kid right there in the snow. Cut it right out of the mother's stomach. I tried to get a better look, but that bossy cop pushed me away. Son, it was just about the ugliest thing I've ever seen. It reminded me of the time old Rolf Mathiason fell into the rock crusher. Now, them was the good ol' days out at the pit. Back when we was—"

"Was the cop Dale Weathers?"

"Eh? The weather? It was nasty. Roads were slick as a perch belly."

"Thanks!" I shouted. I decided I'd learned as much as I could and that I wasn't too keen on hearing any more about Rolf, so I reached over, took Waino's hand and shook it. I smiled and thanked Roddy, but pulled my hand away before the big man could give my arm another pumping.

"Mr. Marshall," Roddy asked, "when's the story going to be in the paper?"

"Eh? Diaper? What diaper?" Waino said. "I done told you, Roddy, I didn't have no…"

I waved good-bye and scooted out the door.

I FOUND GLORY in the room across the hall, perched on a bed and surrounded by a gaggle of laughing grand-mothers. She held a sugar cookie in one hand and a Bar-bie in the other.

The nurse saw me and told the ladies it was time to go. They sighed, took turns hugging Glory—the ones who could reach her—and dispersed while the nurse picked Glory from the bed.

Missy Blue wheeled over to me, pressed a ten-dollar bill into my hand and said, "Buy your daughter some clean pajamas."

FORTY-SEVEN

GLORY LIKED ELMER Alfred Wright the minute I carried her through the door with tinkling bells.

"Vince!" the jovial man yelled as we entered. "I'm so glad you stopped by. Not too surprised, either. And you brought me a little visitor. Who's this?"

The same big-band music filled the showroom. I set Glory down and reached for Wright's offered hand.

"This is Glory. She's helping me today."

"How exciting. I've had quite a lonely day. Not a single customer. And I am in need of a little person to help me. Wait here just a moment please."

Wright disappeared behind a display of walkers and returned with a wheelchair.

"Would you like to test this for me, Glory?"

Glory's eyes widened and her mouth opened into a broad grin as she went for the chair.

"You have excellent timing, Mr. Wright. We came here from Lakeview, and a lady there captivated Glory with her wheelchair and her doll collection."

"That had to be Missy Blue," Wright said. I nodded confirmation. "A fine lady. Very interesting. She loves children. Did you know she can predict the future?"

I laughed and while placing Glory in the chair's seat I

said we hadn't learned that. The chair had a safety strap and I buckled Glory in.

"May I drive?" Wright asked Glory. She nodded her head. Wright began wheeling her around the store, humming and turning like he was dancing to the music. They circled past the counter and returned.

"I suspect you're here about Helen."

"The police told me she's missing."

"The police?" he asked and stopped pushing, a note of concern in his voice. "They're looking for her?"

"Elk Ridge security reported her as missing. The county Search and Rescue team are out in the woods looking for her."

"Goodness, they won't find her there."

Wright started forward, weaving in and out between oxygen bottles, crutches and canvas laundry carts.

"I see. So you know where she is?"

Wright considered this as he did a few pirouettes with Glory.

"No."

"Oh," I said. "When you said they won't find her, I assumed... I hope she's okay."

"I'm pretty sure she's fine," Wright said, now breathing hard. He stopped in front of me. Sweat glistened on his head. "Your turn to push."

"I don't understand." I grabbed the handles and emulated Wright's dance moves. Glory laughed and kicked her feet. She glanced up at me. I saw the twinkle I used to see in Deb's eyes.

"How could I know she's fine? Because I helped her

get away, of course. I suppose you'll pester me for the details until I spill the beans."

"Probably."

"Then I'll share what I know." Wright wiped his head with a handkerchief. "Trusting, of course, that I have your word this stays between the three of us."

"It does." Then I stopped talking and stopped pushing Glory. "Mr. Wright, I can't promise that if she's involved in the death of Vanessa Grey."

"Hmm. I see your point."

Glory tugged my hand. She wanted more ride. I pushed her around the room again. This time I pretended to bump things before veering away.

"Sorry," I said.

"Quite all right. I don't know anything about Vanessa Grey's death, but I think some things are better left un-said. The details are unimportant anyway, just made a good story to tell. Cloak-and-dagger stuff. Sneaking off the property, catching a ride with a friend to town, escaping into the night. That sort of business. Guess I'll have to keep it all to myself. Suffice it to say, Helen learned of something quite terrible."

"What?"

"Oh, she wouldn't share that with me, though I was relentless in my probing. But I believe it's something that happened a long time ago, and Helen recently learned of it. She wanted to get away from Elk Ridge as soon as possible."

"Did she think the knowledge put her in danger?"

"I'd say she always seemed a bit afraid of the Baroness and the security staff. But I'm not sure she felt she was in danger. It was more that she was angry. She did say something about making things right, but wouldn't elaborate."

"And you don't know where she is? Or how I might get in touch with her?"

"I honestly don't," Wright said. "She said she planned to disappear."

FORTY-EIGHT

I CARRIED GLORY through our front door and tiptoed across the soiled carpet. After giving her diaper a quick sniff test, I lay her in her crib. She'd fallen asleep in the Bronco soon after leaving EA Wright, almost as I buckled her car seat.

I smoothed her hair and smiled. As crazy as this day had been, I felt we had some good moments together. Maybe I could get into this fatherhood thing.

I found Deb at the kitchen table, staring out the window at the low whitecaps rolling and breaking on the beach.

"I expected you home before me," Deb said.

"Sorry. I ran a few errands. If I told you about it, you'd get mad."

"You went to work?"

"Dressed like this and with Glory still in pajamas? I don't think so. Besides, I wouldn't want to butt heads with Mort Maki right now." I grabbed the bowls and plates from the floor, where Glory had dropped them in the morning, thinking it wasn't like Deb to have left them. While returning them to the dishwasher, I said, "I didn't think I was going to survive this morning with

Glory. She was out of control from the moment you left. I even tried calling my mom for help."

"I was wondering," Deb said. "What happened in the living room?"

I grabbed Glory's sippy cup from the counter and rinsed it.

"Like I said, things were out of control." I sat across the table from her. "How was the meeting with Sarah?"

"She said they don't have much of a case against Tony—"

I slapped the table a bit more forcefully than I'd meant, rattling silverware and drawing an angry look from Deb. "I don't give a rat's patootie about Tony. What about you?"

"As I was saying, there's a problem with the search. Sarah said that unless there's some other evidence that we don't know about, this case is going nowhere. She went back to represent Tony at his arraignment after we met."

"Great for Tony. Now, what about you?"

Tears welled in her eyes. "Other than being arrested and losing my job, well, I guess I'm doing okay."

"Losing your job? What are you talking about? They can't fire you."

"Tell the school board that. Lucy Demott left a message on our answering machine. She wants me to call her back and comment on my suspension without pay. She said the school board decided in special session this afternoon that I would be a bad influence on the students. They didn't even have the courtesy to call me before telling a TV reporter."

I remembered seeing the cars and people outside the superintendent's office. "I'm really sorry, Deb." I came around the table. "You didn't call her, did you?"

"I think I've had enough publicity for one day." She wiped her eyes and nose with a napkin from the table. "The union steward called a few minutes ago and confirmed it. He said the suspension was until the court decided the case. We'll be paid retroactively if we're cleared."

"Even though you weren't charged?"

"Yes."

"That's crazy, Deb. We'll talk to Sarah about it. They can't do that."

"I'm off the bargaining committee, too," she said. She pushed me back and wiped the tears now rolling down her cheeks. "It looks like the teachers are so embarrassed they're going to set up a new committee and just accept the board's offer. All that work…"

"It isn't going to happen, Deb," I said, wrapping my arms around her. "I promise you that. It isn't going to happen."

"It's just so unfair."

The doorbell rang, startling both of us. I figured it was probably either Lucy or Mort, and I moved to the front room to take a peek. The last person I'd expected to see was Tony Wittmer.

FORTY-NINE

I WAS OUT THE DOOR and backing him down the porch steps with finger jabs to his chest.

"You've caused enough problems. Get the heck out of here."

"I'm really sorry about this," he said, raising his hands in surrender.

"Sorry doesn't cut it. You have three seconds to get off my property before I—"

"Stop it, Vince," Deb said. She came out the door and put a restraining hand on my shoulder.

"Vince, if you want to help Deb, you've got to—"

"You must be using drugs as well as selling them if you think I've got to do anything you say." I enjoyed seeing Tony wince. Deb tightened her hand.

"Vince," she said, "remember what I told you earlier, about this being a setup? Please listen to what he has to say."

I whirled around. "This is ludicrous. This is the guy who—"

"Who you think I've been having an affair with?"

"He's gotten you thrown in jail, suspended from your job and, yes, I think he's gotten a little too friendly."

"I—" Tony said.

I whirled back toward Wittmer and shouted, "You get outta—"

"—I'm gay."

"—here."

I stared at Wittmer, turned to Deb and saw her nod.

"What the—?" I'm sure I looked a bit stupid staring from one to the other, my jaw hanging open. "Yeah, right," I said. "So what. It doesn't make a bit of difference."

"He's only telling you so that you'll give up the bone-headed notion that we're romantically involved, Vince. We need you on our side and you need to start thinking clearly. It's time to trust me again, Vince."

"Gay? As in…?"

Wittmer nodded.

I turned to Deb and asked, "How come I didn't know this?"

"Because normally my personal life is nobody's business," Wittmer said. "Deb's right, I'm only telling you so you can get past thinking we're having an affair."

"I still can't understand why you're sticking your neck out for him, Deb. What about the drugs? What about your job?"

"What I've been trying to tell you is that Tony didn't cause this trouble. The person who planted the drugs did."

I groaned. "Right. I just don't get it. The cops have already let you off. It's his problem now."

Deb and Tony exchanged a glance, then he looked down and shoved his hands into his coat pockets.

"It's because he's my friend. Isn't that enough?"

"Some friend," I said.

"Yes, he is," she said, and this time she poked her finger at me. "Tony helped me once and it cost him his job. I owe him."

"You don't owe me anything," Wittmer said.

"Back in Grand Rapids, three students cornered me in an empty hallway and threatened me. They were grabbing and pushing, being real jerks. I lost control of the situation. They knew I was scared."

"You never told me this."

"Of course not," Deb said. "You'd have made a federal case out of it. And we were already planning to move here anyway. I just wanted it to go away."

I couldn't believe I hadn't known this.

"Things were getting out of hand until Tony showed up. He pulled them away from me. They threatened him. He subdued one of the kids while the other two ran. Later, all three were expelled. It was kept quiet, done in a closed school-board session. Remember when I had to attend those few meetings right before we left Grand Rapids?"

"So I guess I owe you thanks, Wittmer," I said. "But I don't see how that could cost you your job."

"Two years after you left," Wittmer said, "one of those kids found out about my personal life. HIs family made it their mission to embarrass me and tried to get the school board to fire me. The board, of course, didn't respond, but the publicity was unbearable for me. I had no private life. I lost my partner over it. So I cut a deal with the school to leave. They guaranteed good references and gave me a cash buyout. I took a year off, did some traveling, but missed the teaching."

"He contacted me after that," Deb said. "I encouraged him to apply at Bay High. That's why he moved here."

I leaned back and studied Wittmer a few moments.

"Gordon Greenleaf told me there was something fishy about why you left the job in Grand Rapids. He was looking into it."

"Now you know. He won't get any information from the school, unless they break our agreement."

"There's no other reason?" I asked. "Nothing to do with…with students?"

"Vince," Deb said, "how could you ask that?"

"Mort implied that Tony has a reputation for dating much younger people—as in high-school age. He said you're running around with girl students, but he could have misunderstood his source, not realized it was boys."

"Mort's full of it," Deb said.

"Vince, I'm gay, not a pedophile."

"Okay, so maybe I've been a tiny bit of an idiot," I said. "Let's go inside and you tell me your conspiracy theory. It sounds like listening is the least I can do considering what Deb says you've done for her."

"THE LAST TIME I checked my trunk, it was empty," Wittmer said. We were sitting around the kitchen table, since the living room was still a repository of potting soil. "And the cops, I mean, get real. They follow us all over town, then stop us and ask me to pop the trunk. What's up with that? They obviously knew what was in there."

"I know this sounds crazy," Deb said, "but we're pretty sure we know who did it and why."

"Go on," I said.

"Ken Romano," they said in unison.

As soon as she said the name, it clicked in place for me: The debts, the valedictorian scheme, seeing him in the Ramada hallway the previous night.

"His shop serviced my car yesterday," Wittmer said. "I saw Ken Junior in the shop when I picked it up. I think either he or his father planted the drugs to disrupt the contract negotiations."

"And he's been successful," Deb said.

"The thing I can't understand is why he put so much in the trunk," Wittmer said. "It must have cost him a bundle. He could have accomplished the same thing with a little baggie."

"I think I might have the answer to that," I said.

FIFTY

I DROVE THROUGH twilight to Gordon Greenleaf's house.
A half-moon hung over Superior, looking mammoth in
the low horizon. It lay a silver path on the lake. I always
enjoy the drive to Greenleaf's because the road hugs
the lakeshore for three miles north of Apostle Bay before turning inland. The lake seems like the end of the
world here, the infinite horizon broken only by the occasional ore ship heading northwest toward Duluth or
east to the Soo.

A mile beyond where the road moved away from the
lake, I turned left onto a narrow asphalt drive. When the
pavement ended, I slowed and turned onto the property
Greenleaf inherited from his parents. On most nights,
only owl hoots, coyote yips and, in May, the incessant
chirping of peepers disturb the night. Every now and
then a four-wheeler drones on distant logging roads, the
sound buffered by the forest.

I bounced down a short dirt drive and into a well-lit
gravel parking area in front of Greenleaf's cabin. The
detective shared his log home with two dogs: A decrepit
beagle, now lolling on the porch edge; and a yellow Lab
puppy, leaping like a gazelle near my door.

Greenleaf was leaning back in a rocking chair on the

cabin's porch. His feet rested on the timber rail. The detective wore jeans, hooded sweatshirt and running shoes. He stood when I approached and told his Lab, Sheila, to relax. Then he showed me a brown bottle and offered to get me a beer. When I declined, he sat back down and waved toward the adjacent rocking chair.

"Beautiful night," Greenleaf said. "Fall is the best time here—no bugs, and mild weather."

"Yep," I said. I scratched Sheila's head. Then I bent and patted the old beagle named Ralph. The dog opened one eye in acknowledgment, then went comatose again.

I settled into the rocker. "Thanks for letting me come over and bother you. I appreciate it."

"You'd have harassed me until I did. I figured I'd save myself the trouble."

"You don't think Wittmer's the guy, either, do you?"

He shrugged. "The more I think about it, the more questions I have."

"Did you learn anything from Grand Rapids?"

"Yes," Greenleaf said and paused to sip his beer. "Nothing relating to drugs."

"You get that from the school?"

"The PD. He left the school for other reasons."

"Because he's homosexual," I said. "It's not public knowledge. He'd like to keep it that way."

Greenleaf nodded again, sipped his beer, then said, "The anonymous tip worries me. It was too easy."

"Just like the kids you arrested? I think you had it right the first time."

"Maybe. Something's still missing."

"I checked the court records. Ken Romano has trouble paying his bills."

Greenleaf stopped rocking and put his legs down on the deck. "What did you find?"

"Two lawsuits. He owes money, and he's strapped for cash. He isn't paying his employees' health-insurance premiums."

"Interesting," Greenleaf said.

"Did Wittmer tell you he had his car serviced at Romano Auto Sales yesterday?"

Greenleaf nodded.

"You might want to check his trunk for prints. Who knows whose fingers have been touching it?"

"Vince, it's already in the works," Greenleaf said. "Give me some credit, will you?"

"I'm going to Ken Romano's. You want to come?"

"You're not going there. I'll talk to the chief about this in the morning. See what he thinks. We'll probably bring Romano in for a chat. You go home and get some sleep. I'll call you tomorrow."

"Suit yourself." I stood.

"Don't do it, Vince."

"I have to."

"You'll blow the case."

"What I'm going to blow is the story on this. This creep has done enough to Deb. It's payback time."

"You're just trying to make up for your own blunders here, Vince. Let us do it. If he's behind it, he'll go down."

"See ya," I said, standing and then walking off the porch.

"Vince, you're nuts."

"Maybe." I kept moving toward my Bronco, ignoring Sheila's spastic leaps in front of me.

"Then wait up, you idiot. I'm coming, too."

GREENLEAF DROVE HIS OWN CAR, and he insisted on leading. I followed him along the lakeshore. The moon looked smaller now that it had risen above the horizon. Its silver reflection showed a lake as smooth as polished granite.

Greenleaf drove into Apostle Bay, past the *Chronicle* and other downtown buildings, and through to the south side of town. We stopped at a traffic light near the ore dock. I noticed a jacked-up red four-wheel-drive pickup idling in the opposite lane. When the light changed, the truck squealed rubber and roared through the intersection. I watched it, thinking something about the truck was familiar, until the car behind me honked.

Ahead of me, Greenleaf was pulling away, his blue dash-mounted light now flashing. I looked down and realized I'd left the scanner off, so I flipped it on and punched the accelerator.

"—fire at 1827 Sunnybrook Drive."

Romano's house.

I followed Greenleaf into the neighborhood, blew past a stop sign and squealed around the corner. Two blocks ahead, flames leaped through the upper-story windows of a white Cape Cod. Greenleaf slid to a stop in front of the home. As I pulled in behind him, I saw a man hobbling toward Greenleaf and waving his arms frantically.

Firelight reflected on the white cast wrapping the man's leg, turning it orange.

I grabbed my camera and tape recorder and clicked the recorder on. That was something Lou taught me: Always have the recorder on, because you never know what you'll get on tape.

Then I ran toward the house. Romano met me in the yard. I didn't see Greenleaf.

"You have to help him!" Romano shouted. "My son is trapped in there." Romano grabbed my shoulders with both hands. Tears poured down his cheeks. "My son. Oh, God, I can't believe what I've done. You have to get him out."

"Is there anyone else in there?" I asked. "Did Gordon go inside?" I noticed the front door stood open.

"It's all my fault. If I hadn't been so stupid," Romano sobbed. He collapsed on the ground at my feet.

I grabbed him by the arm and jerked him up. "Did Gordon go inside?" I shouted. "Is there anyone else in there?"

In the distance, sirens screamed, the sound rising as it entered the neighborhood. I noticed neighbors standing nearby, watching the flames and pointing.

"I just wanted to get out of the red," Romano moaned. "That's all I wanted to do. But when I lost that shipment, those guys went crazy. They're maniacs."

I scanned the house. Flames sprang from all the first-story windows now, and smoke leaked through the siding. The heat reached out, hitting us, blowing our hair back. I dragged Romano further away.

"What are you talking about?" I shouted.

"Those two rednecks from Eden—they broke my leg and trashed my dealership. They did this." He waved at the house. "It's my payback for losing their precious, stinking marijuana. All I wanted to do was get out of the hole." Romano buried his face in his hands. I let go of his arm, and he slumped onto the ground. "Oh, God, my son is in there."

I moved toward the house, but the heat pushed me back, robbed my breath. I lifted the camera and snapped a few pictures.

Fire engines roared onto the front lawn and I heard shouting. A second-floor window opened. I aimed my camera at the window. Smoke billowed through now; great black, roiling clouds. A moment later a body went over the sill. It inched down, then I saw a soot-stained Greenleaf hanging on to the body's arms, swinging it out and dropping the person away from the house. I shot photos until a fireman came into view, grabbed the body and pulled it away.

Greenleaf disappeared back inside. Then I saw him climb onto the sill and, in one smooth motion, jump. I ran toward him, but a firefighter yanked me back.

"Out of the way!" he shouted.

I struggled but couldn't break the man's grip. Two firefighters scooped Greenleaf off the ground and carried him away from the house. The firefighter shoved me back and someone else grabbed me.

"Get any good pictures?" Dale Weathers shouted into my ear.

"Chief!"

Weathers started toward the fire trucks, one firm hand still on my arm.

"I know who did this," I called after him.

"Speak up," Weathers said, without slowing his pace.

I explained about the jacked-up pickup I'd seen peeling away from the stoplight and reminded him it sounded like the truck in the vandalism report from Romano's dealership. Weathers brought his radio up to his mouth and spoke to dispatch. By the time he finished, we were next to Greenleaf. The detective sucked oxygen from a mask. An EMT had cut away his shirt and was dressing burns on his arm. The stink of burnt hair and smoke made me want to gag.

"How you doing, son?" Weathers asked Greenleaf.

Greenleaf pulled the mask back. "Been worse."

"That took guts," Weathers said. He asked the EMT, "How's the kid?"

"Burns and smoke inhalation," the EMT said. "But he'll survive."

Weathers nodded, then turned to me. "Coming here tonight was stupid."

"Chief—"

"But it saved the kid's life. Gordon called me on his way here. He told me your theory. I want to hear it myself."

"How about I let you hear it in Romano's own words?" I said. I held up the recorder.

FIFTY-ONE

"GORDO, DID YOU BUY real coffee filters or something?" I sat in my usual seat—the one Deb had been sitting in less than twenty-four hours earlier. "This brew almost tastes good."

"It's the same old stuff," the detective said. "I thought you were supposed to be taking a few days off."

"And miss this? I don't think so."

Greenleaf leaned forward and eased his bandaged arms onto the desk surface. Gauze, wrapped from wrist to elbow, covered second- and third-degree burns. He sported a buzz cut now, hidden under a ball cap. A nurse had shorn the burnt hair from his head last night at the hospital. His eyebrows were gone, fried by the fire.

I sipped the foam cup of coffee again, set it on Greenleaf's desk and opened my notebook.

"Seriously, Gordon, how are you feeling this morning? Like a hero?"

"Like a goofy teenager who fell asleep on the beach. Remember those days, when we'd see who could burn the reddest?"

"Young and stupid. Now we're older and, well… Are you sure you're okay? How are the ankles?"

"Fine. I'm sore, but fine."

"It was nuts to go into that house. The heat was so intense I couldn't bear it, and I was twenty yards away."

"I went in before the fire got bad. You'd have done the same."

I thought about that. I'd been thinking about it most of the night, and I was ashamed by the answer I kept finding. "Doubtful," I said.

"You do what you have to do."

"How did it go with Romano last night?"

"The chief let him ride with his son to the hospital and stayed with him until he knew the kid was out of danger. Afterward, Ken spilled his guts."

"He admitted planting the weed in Tony Wittmer's car?"

"Nope. He didn't plant the stuff."

"What?"

Greenleaf grabbed his cup, a royal-blue ceramic mug with the Apostle Bay PD insignia. He held it toward me and smiled.

"How about a refill?" he asked.

I stood from the chair, grabbed the coffeepot in the office corner and poured. Still standing, I said, "Are you going to tell me or make me drag it out of you?"

"Ken lost the marijuana. That's why the Eden boys were harassing him. He couldn't pay, and he couldn't return the goods. By the way, state police caught those boys. You guessed right on that. They were halfway back to the peninsula when a patrol car spotted their truck and called in reinforcements. The boys"—Greenleaf paused and looked through a report on his desk—"twins John and Jerrod Gustafson, age twenty-eight, led 'em on a wild chase through some logging roads before losing it on a turn and wrapping their pickup around a tree.

"A couple of people in Romano's neighborhood saw their red truck," Greenleaf continued. "Witnesses said the truck drove onto Romano's lawn and the Gustafsons tossed a couple of Molotov cocktails at the house. I'm not sure if they meant to burn the place or scare Romano, but one went through a window and I guess it spread pretty fast."

"You'd think they'd drive a nondescript truck if they planned on torching someone's home."

"That's the one advantage police down in the Eden area have. Honest farmers drive beat-up old pickups. The few bad apples in the drug trade can't help showing off all the money they're making."

"Boneheads."

"Now that we have a description of them, we'll hopefully find a couple of more witnesses who saw them at the dealership."

"So, if Ken Senior lost the pot, who had it?"

"His kid. Junior confessed this morning, once he heard what his father told us. Seems he found the stash hidden at the dealership while he was putting in time at the service department. Ken Junior thought the weed belonged to an employee, so he took it and hid the stuff in a storage locker."

"Right under his father's nose?"

"Yep. A little bit later he got the bright idea to discredit his classmates."

"Your valedictorian theory was right?"

"Sad, isn't it? He claimed his dad had been pressuring him about being first in his class, and he couldn't take it. He admitted to framing the other students. We already knew he was the anonymous tipster. After we arrested him—that wasn't in his plan—he decided it was getting dangerous and tried to unload the stuff. Junior contacted an old school chum who had moved to Green Bay and tried to set up the buy. When that fell through, he decided to ditch the marijuana, and he saw a perfect chance to help his dad, too. Seems that Ken Senior was badmouthing Wittmer for several weeks about the teacher negotiations. Ken Junior planted the stuff in Wittmer's car when it was in for service."

"He tipped you off, too?"

"Worked for him before," Greenleaf said.

"Thanks for keeping all this from the television news last night," I said. "I appreciate your letting the newspaper have the first report."

"Not my doing, I was, uh, detained. Besides, we didn't keep this from anyone. Most of it was learned in the wee hours." Greenleaf leaned back into his chair again, bringing his mug with him. "Maybe it was a good thing you talked me into going there last night. But I hope you don't use this as a reason to go off half-cocked again next time."

"You know me, Gord. Mister Cooperation," I said, lifting my cup in salute.

He rolled his eyes.

"I READ YOUR STORIES," Lou Kendricks growled when I walked into the newsroom. "I put some notes on your computer, things that need clarification." Kendricks remained hunched over his keyboard and didn't look at me as he said this. "Get on it right away. When Maki gets in, he'll need your help. His school-board story says Deb and that other guy were suspended without pay. I'm guessing that will change after last night. And I want anything mentioning your wife or Tony Wittmer moved into his story, not under your byline."

"Sorry, but I can't help you, Lou." I slid behind my desk and saw my story about Greenleaf rescuing Ken Junior on the monitor. Lou's comments blazed in a red font at the screen's top. "I'm on vacation, remember? Publisher's orders."

Kendricks snorted. "Reporters are never on vacation. Get to work. Oh"—and for the first time, he looked up and caught my eyes—"excellent art. We're going to run at least three of your photos. It's going to be a killer front page today."

"Thanks. You think we can squeeze in another piece?"

"Don't get greedy."

"Because those kids from Bay High, the ones convicted of marijuana possession this summer, they've been exonerated. Ken Romano Junior confessed this morning to setting them up."

"You get that from Rudy Clark?"

"From the cops. But believe me, I will enjoy calling Mr. Prosecutor and getting his comment."

Kendricks chuckled. "We'll find a way to fit it on the page. Don't rub Clark's face in it too much." He paused, sipped his coffee, then said, "On second thought, give him a little heat. He deserves it."

I smiled, rested my fingers on the keyboard and paused. Had it really been only two days since I'd last written here?

I READ THROUGH Lou's comments and reworked the story, adding the note about police arresting the arson suspects. I opened the story about Ken Romano's confession and added new details I'd learned that morning from Greenleaf. Halfway through the story, I read about Romano's court troubles and remembered my deal with Monty Haver. I'd better walk over to the courthouse after deadline and give him enough gossip to get Apostle Bay buzzing for a few weeks.

"CAN'T YOU STAY out of the news for one day, Marshall?" asked Mort Maki. He walked by my desk and tossed his briefcase down. "I'm tired of writing about you and your family."

"Maybe if you got the story right the first time you wouldn't have to do it anymore."

"Knock it off, you two," Kendricks said. He rolled his chair over to Maki's desk. "You both have a load to do this morning, and you have to work together. Vince, brief Maki on what you know. Maki, the teacher story needs rewriting."

"What's wrong with it?" Maki said as he peeled off his coat and reached for his lunch bag. "You want me to add something about Romano's house catching on fire? Do the cops think the teachers did it?"

Kendricks stared at Maki a moment, then shook his head and rolled back to his desk.

"Ken confessed to being Apostle Bay's own drug kingpin last night," I said. I made a halfhearted attempt to keep the smirk off my face. "Oh, and his son planted the marijuana in Tony Wittmer's car."

Maki stopped digging for his lunch and dropped into his chair. "You're kidding."

"Scout's honor. Wittmer's been cleared. Two Romanos will be facing the judge—one when he gets out of the hospital."

"Oh, man," Maki whined. "They didn't say anything about this on the television. I'm going to have to do a total rewrite and call everyone again."

"Let me help you. I have Deb's phone number for you right here."

FIFTY-TWO

KENDRICKS SENT THE FRONT PAGE to the press and I walked to the Superior County Courthouse. I found Monty Haver climbing from a dazzling white Navigator, parked at the building's upper entrance in the spot reserved for the clerk. Haver wore black slacks and a black silk shirt open at the neck.

"What do you think?" Haver said when he saw me. He raised his arms, the right hand holding a small leather briefcase, and turned in a circle.

"Nice clothes," I said.

"Not the clothes. Do I look slimmer? I've dropped fifteen pounds."

"In two days?"

"Sure. It's the new me."

I couldn't tell the difference but was glad to see him smiling.

"Heading to your office?" I asked. "I have news."

"About last night, I'm sure. Something juicy?"

"Beyond juicy."

"Ooh, I like that. Let's get Rhonda."

I followed Haver through the county building's large oak doors and into the clerk's office. Haver held the swinging panel at the counter open and invited me into his sanctum. We found Rhonda Wentworth already there, directing a young female custodian on how to polish the wainscoting.

"Always buff with the wood grain," Wentworth said. "Make sure you only use soft rags."

She saw me, then looked at Marty.

"Do we need some privacy?" Wentworth asked.

"Might be prudent," Haver said. "Mr. Marshall has something of great importance to tell us. I believe he called it 'beyond juicy.'"

"Why don't you come back to this later?" Rhonda said. She took the custodian by the arm and guided her into the outer office. There, she asked the woman to sweep behind the counter. Rhonda returned and closed the door. She perched on Haver's desk. "She's new," Rhonda said, nodding at the door. "A single mom. I think a judge found her the job after seeing her in court."

"So what big news do you bring us?" Haver asked. "This is, I expect, your part of our bargain."

"It is," I said. I told them the Romano story. As I did, I could see Monty and Rhonda fidgeting. The two couldn't sit still.

"It seems the information you found in our records was the key," Haver said after I finished answering their questions. I watched Rhonda slide off the desk and move toward the door.

"It was. I wouldn't have connected it without seeing those KRI files. I'm personally grateful because that information saved my wife's reputation."

"I believe it also saved Ken Romano Junior's life,"

Haver said. He beamed as if he'd pulled the kid from the fire himself. In a small way he had, I thought.

"I have some calls to make," Rhonda said. She was hopping like she needed to use the restroom. She walked out, leaving the door open behind her.

"She has to start the grapevine," Haver said. "Being first is important."

"I suppose you have things to do also." I stood. "Thanks again for your help."

"Anytime. Glad to be of service," Haver said. "If you ever need anything else, just let me know."

I smiled and walked out of the office. Haver was talking on the phone by the time I reached the counter: "You won't believe this…"

I walked further into the courthouse, thinking I'd stop by Rudy Clark's office. The prosecutor hadn't returned my calls that morning. Instead, the little chicken had faxed a statement to the newspaper. Clark's quote, which I paraphrased because it was so outlandish, made it sound like his decision to cut a deal with Ken Junior was part of a grand plan to smoke out the real villain. There was no mention of an apology to the other seven kids he'd erroneously prosecuted.

Guess that's the downside of prosecutors being elected officials, I thought. It turns some of them into politicians.

I ambled toward the rotunda, the central part of the county building. When I reached the circle, I stopped in the center and gazed at the judge portraits: All gruff and distinguished men, staring off into the distance with haughty, upturned chins. I had known two of them per-sonally—one a rabid Green Bay Packers fan who spent every autumn Sunday in our home watching the games with my dad. Those men weren't gruff or haughty at all. Too bad history would remember them that way. It made me realize Patrice was right: You've got to go at things from several angles to get the true story.

Footsteps echoing on the marble floor interrupted that thought. I saw the chief marching toward me, lost in his own concerns.

"Hey, Chief."

"Oh." Dale Weathers looked startled. "Hello."

He stopped next to me, put his hand on my shoulder.

"Are you coming from Clark's office?" I asked.

He grunted. "That man's insufferable."

"Yep," I agreed, a bit surprised at the chief's frank words. "Gordon told me about the confessions. Thanks for keeping it under wraps until this morning."

"We didn't do it as a favor to you or Kendricks," he said. "I'd sit on the information until the arraignment if the news wasn't already common knowledge."

"Thanks anyway, Chief."

"You know I don't approve of what you did last night. You could have blown the investigation."

"I know, but—"

Weathers interrupted, "Your father would be proud."

We stood in silence for a moment, staring at the im-perious faces.

Weathers broke the spell. "I have to get going."

"Chief, there's something I've been meaning to ask you."

"Yes?" He was poised to walk away.

I swallowed. I'd wanted to ask him this question for two days, and now that I had the man, it was hard to spit the words out.

"Yes?" Weathers asked, a note of impatience entering his voice.

"Tell me what happened at that car accident thirty-two years ago," I blurted out. "The night Autumn Coyote and William Pontcliff died. I know you were there. Dad was, too."

Weathers went pale. He opened his mouth and the lips moved, but no words came out. He blinked, looked away and composed himself.

"Why can't you give this up?" he asked.

"What happened to their baby?"

Weathers coughed. Still looking away, he said, "I can't talk about it."

"Can't or won't?"

"Can't."

"Did Dad make a mistake that night? Are you and Mom trying to cover for him?"

Weathers turned back, his eyes as hard and polished as agate from Lake Superior.

"Your father didn't make any mistakes that night. But if you pursue this further, you will."

The chief turned and walked out of the rotunda. I stared after him, wondering what he meant. I kept staring until the dark, oaken barriers swung shut behind him.

Then an idea struck and I jogged back to Haver's office.

Rhonda Wentworth sat at her desk in the outer office, whispering into her phone. I waited a few moments for her to notice me, then gave up and passed behind the counter. I knocked and pushed Haver's massive office door open enough to look inside. Haver was talking into the phone, too, his back to the door, looking through the office windows at the sparse morning traffic filtering through Apostle Bay.

Haver must have sensed me, because he turned, looked surprised, then waved me in. I waited for him to complete the call. By the time Haver and Wentworth had finished their telephoning, half of Apostle Bay would run for the *Chronicle*'s news stands. Maybe Lou Kendricks should give the clerk's office a share of the day's profits, I thought.

Haver hung up. "Don't tell me there's more to the story."

"No. Not yet anyway. I meant to ask you something earlier. Can I look up a birth certificate?"

Haver leaned back in his chair and folded his jumbo hands across his belly.

"Depends on whose it is. You can look up yours and your immediate family's. Under certain circumstances, we'll let you look up various ancestors for genealogical searches—if they've been dead awhile."

"I need to find out about a non-relative."

"Not possible."

"You remember the woman who died jumping off Eagle's Cliff?" I then told an abbreviated version of the story. When I'd completed it, I said, "I'm trying to find if that child lived."

"And then what?" Haver asked.

"What do you mean?"

"Suppose the child lived. You find out his or her name. What are you going to do then?"

"I don't know. I hadn't thought that far yet."

"Exactly. What if the child doesn't want to know? He or she is in their thirties now. What if they have a happy life? How would you feel if one day someone came along and told you that's how you were born? It would turn your life upside down."

"C'mon, Monty. If the child lived, the Grey family raised him or her somewhere far from here. I'd never find the person. Besides, it's not the child I'm that interested in. It's my father and how he was involved that night. Listen, before April Coyote died, she said my father killed her sister and the child. I know he wouldn't have done that, but I need to know if something bad happened."

Haver turned and looked out his windows again. I waited. I looked at my watch and I waited. I wondered if Haver had drifted off.

The big man turned.

"I can't look up someone else's birth certificate for you. I'm sorry."

I held the man's eyes a moment, then looked at the floor. So that's the end of the road, I thought.

I stood. Haver apologized again. I moved toward the door, then turned.

"If I gave you the date, could you do me a favor? Just look it up and see if there was a child born. I don't need to see the name or anything. I just want to know if the child lived. It would erase any doubts."

Haver considered this a moment. Then he leaned forward and grabbed his computer mouse. "What's the date? I'll look it up myself. I'll tell you if someone was born on that date and nothing more—if I can find it. And that's a big *if.* The records are supposed to be all cross-referenced in our system, but there are lots of gaps from the pre-computer days."

I gave him the date and he searched with a series of clicks. I dropped into the chair, watched him tap a few keys and waited. After a few moments he looked over and gave me an angry stare, then clicked his mouse once more and studied the screen another moment.

"Is this your idea of a bad joke?" Haver asked. Something had happened, because he looked furious.

"No. What are you talking about?"

Haver looked back and forth from the screen to me, and his face hardened in a way I had never seen before.

"What is it, Monty?"

"No joke?"

"No, why?"

He stayed silent, contemplating something, then cleared his screen and stood.

"I'll be back in a moment," he said.

As his office door swung shut behind him, my cell phone rang. I grabbed it and saw my home number on the screen.

"Hi, Deb."

"Hi. I tried you at the office and you weren't there." She was breathless.

"I'm at the courthouse. Have you heard from the school yet?"

"The superintendent called," she said. I heard Glory singing in the background. "The school board reinstated both Tony and me. I think the board's embarrassed and may even accept our latest contract offer—just to get this out of the news."

"Great. That's wonderful. I'll come home for lunch and we can celebrate."

"That sounds good. Oh, I found that missing mail. It was under a couch cushion. There's a letter for you."

"Oh, wow, I forgot all about that. Can you please open it? I need to know what it says."

"I guess. Is it so important that it can't wait until you get home?" There was a teasing note in her voice.

"It might be."

"Okay. It's in the kitchen. I'll call you back in a few minutes."

"Thanks."

I ended the call, then stood to check on Haver and almost collided with the big man when he pushed through the door. Haver walked past me and slapped the file onto his desk. I wanted to leave, but something in the man's behavior paralyzed me.

Haver sighed. "You can look at it," he said. "But before you do, think very hard about what I said earlier. *Very hard.* Some things are better left alone." Then he turned to the window.

I studied the man's back a moment, waiting to see if he'd add anything else. Then I reached and flipped open the manila folder.

What I saw was surely a mistake.

FIFTY-THREE

A LONE SMOKER stood by the *Chronicle*'s rear entrance, a place where the pressmen normally hang out after the morning's run.

I might have recognized the man's broad shoulders, longish black hair and weathered face had he glanced over. But my mind was on the document in Haver's office and my need to go home.

"Vince Marshall?" the man called.

I moved toward my car and dug keys from my pocket. On some level I heard the voice, but it didn't register until the man called again, this time louder. I turned. For a moment the world kept whirling. I closed my eyes, opened them and focused on the man approaching, the man in jeans and a denim jacket, the man with his hands now in his pants pockets, the cigarette gone.

"Gary Redwing."

I turned back to the Bronco and opened my door.

"I came to see the place," Redwing said.

"What place?" I tossed my notebook across to the passenger seat.

"Where April jumped. You were right. The view's something special."

I climbed into the seat and then I looked back at Redwing.

"That's nice. Look, I'm sorry to blow you off, but I'm in a big hurry."

"Sure. It's just…you said to let you know if I learned anything else."

Redwing's words caught up with my mind about the same time my cell rang again. It was Deb's second try to reach me since leaving the courthouse, but I couldn't answer. I needed to see her in person. I tossed the phone on the passenger seat and stepped from the truck.

"What's up, Gary?"

"I'm April's personal representative, her executor. She had a will. That sure surprised me."

Redwing pulled his hands free, reached inside the denim coat and retrieved a cigarette pack. He shook one free, put it in his mouth and lit it with matches he pulled from the pack's outer lining. I looked at my watch twice while Redwing did this.

"And?" I prompted.

"I rode the bus here yesterday. Not a bad ride," Redwing said and sucked on the cigarette. He exhaled. "I came to get her grandfather's car—her car—from the cops. Guess it's mine now. Never thought I'd own a Cadillac."

"Was there something in the will? Something about Autumn?"

"No." He worked the cigarette again.

Not bothering to mask my exasperation, I said, "You wanted to tell me something."

"I drove to that place this morning—what do you call it, Eagle's Cliff?"

"Uh-huh."

"Then I was on my way home. Picked up a hitch-hiker down the road. A colored kid with strange hair. Just for company."

"Gary, I'm in a big hurry. Can you get to the point?" Redwing dropped the cigarette and ground it with his work boot. He reached into his back pants pocket and pulled out a folded brown envelope.

"About fifty miles south of here I had a flat," Redwing said. "The kid didn't help. He took off into the woods. He wasn't much company."

Redwing transferred the envelope into his left hand. I looked at my watch and considered grabbing the envelope.

"When I pulled the spare out of the trunk, I found this," Redwing said, waving the envelope. "It was under the tire."

"Did April leave it there?"

Redwing shrugged his shoulders. I waited for more, but the big man didn't say anything.

"Gary, what's in the envelope?"

"I'm guessing some of those papers you were looking for. It appears the baby didn't die in the accident."

He moved the envelope toward me.

I stared at the brown parcel resting less than a foot away and couldn't move my hand to take it.

"Take it. Won't do me any good."

I reached up and took the brown package. My fingers

felt numb and I needed to consciously squeeze to keep from dropping the thin package.

"Thanks," I said. The flap was open. I reached in and pulled out three pages. I set the envelope on the Bronco's seat, then blinked and focused on the papers. The top page was a Superior County probate court agreement.

I scanned the text. The document was simple. John Coyote, next of kin to Autumn Coyote, agreed to terminate all claims of guardianship to the unnamed male child born to his daughter. The document was dated a month after the accident that took her life.

I flipped the page. The next document was two pages and filled with legalese, but the gist was plain. For a quarter million dollars, paid by Vanessa Grey, John Coyote agreed to sign the previous document. He also agreed that he'd never make an additional claim against the Grey family. Harlan Montgomery, Grey's attorney, witnessed the document.

So Montgomery knew, too, I thought.

I reread the papers, looking for the child's name, looking for confirmation of what I'd seen in Haver's office, but it wasn't mentioned. I slipped the papers back into the envelope.

"Thank you," I said.

"No problem," Redwing said. "I hope you can track the kid down. Let him know he's a Coyote."

"You can count on it."

I started to climb into the Bronco, but the look in Redwing's eyes stopped me.

"Was there something else?" I asked.

"Eagle's Cliff—it's not the kind of place where she would have killed herself."

Redwing lit another cigarette and walked away.

FIFTY-FOUR

Mom's car was in the driveway, but Deb stood alone on the porch, her puffy, red eyes visible from across the lawn. When I approached she came down the stairs and threw her arms around me.

"I tried calling," she said.

"I know. Where's Glory?"

Deb released me and wiped her eyes. "She's fine. Tony came and took her to the park a few minutes ago"— she reached up and put her hand on my lips, thinking I was going to protest—"because I asked him to."

I nodded agreement.

"Is Mom inside?"

Deb grabbed my arm when I started past. "I read the letter…"

"I'm pretty sure I know what it says." I saw Deb's puzzled look. "It's a long story, Deb. I need to talk with Mom."

We walked through the door. Deb glanced into the empty living room.

"She was just here," Deb said.

"Out there." I pointed toward the kitchen window, to where I could see Mom standing on the beach, her back to the house, her hair dancing in the wind.

"I KNOW THE TRUTH," I said.

Mom still faced Superior, but I knew she'd heard me. I'd seen her flinch when our shoes scraped the rocks, then straighten her broad shoulders as if bracing for a blow. I stared at her back, at the strands of hair flying up off her shoulders, at the way her shoulders rose as she inhaled before speaking. Waiting for her answer, I wanted desperately at that moment to hate her for not telling me, but I couldn't. I couldn't feel anything. It was like a dream.

"Doc brought you home that night," she said. "You were so, so tiny."

She spoke into the wind and her words seemed to blow back at me, as if coming from the lake itself.

"Your father's heart broke when he couldn't save her, Vince. Before she died, he promised he'd take care of you. And he did. He loved you as if his soul's redemption depended on it. In some ways, I think it did."

I remembered the times Dad locked himself away in the study for hours after a patient died and understood what she meant.

"Doc couldn't leave you in the hospital that night, couldn't abandon you in the nursery. He brought you home, and we held you all night. We fed you, swaddled you, sang to you. We knew we couldn't keep you, but... for one night, you were the dream we'd prayed for. For one night, I had a child. And Doc had saved at least some small part of a dying patient.

"Then one night became two. Then a week. We knew

it would end but didn't want it to. All this time, Dale was dealing with the family, with that cruel woman."

"My grandmother," I whispered. It hit me for the first time that I was related to that woman who'd treated me so wickedly a few days ago. She sat in front of me and knew I was her grandson and she didn't say a thing about it.

"A vicious woman who'd rather you had died," Mom whispered. She shivered, as if the Baroness's ghost had reached from the lake and touched her. "She called you a half-breed and demanded we give you to her so she could send you to an orphanage, a place far away, where you could never learn who you were."

"You kept it from me anyway," I said, at first not realizing I'd spoken the words aloud.

She turned slowly toward me, as if straining against some unseen force.

"We had to. Don't you understand? We had to keep it from you." Tears welled from her eyes, cascaded down her flushed, wind-burned cheeks. "It was the only way she finally agreed to let us adopt you. We promised that we'd never tell you. And if you found out on your own, even if it was beyond our control, she said she'd take you back and punish you somehow. She reached across the table in that fake castle of hers and poked her bony finger into Doc's chest and promised that you'd have a life of misery if you ever found out."

I remembered that night she was so close to my face. I smelled her cloying perfume again, and I recalled how she poked her finger at me, too. Her words made sense now that there was no senility in them as Montgomery implied.

"But after I was an adult, what then? She couldn't put me in an orphanage then."

"Oh, she knew that, too. She and her lawyers worked that out."

Mom turned back to Superior.

"She bought our silence," she said, the words trailing off.

"How much?" Then I shouted, "How much was I worth? A quarter million? That's what she paid John Coyote. Was it enough that you pushed April Coyote over the edge to keep her silent?"

When she turned, her hand came up in a blur and smacked me before I could react. The slap sent me backward, stumbling over a rock, and I fell on the sand.

Mom gasped. "I'm sorry."

"It wasn't suicide," I said.

"No. It was stupidity."

"Please. We've come this far. Tell me what really happened."

"She was drunk. I guess she'd followed me out to Eagle's Cliff that morning. And when I'd set up my easel, she came at me, screaming that your father had killed her sister. She slurred her words and I didn't understand what she was saying at first. She was out of control. She stumbled over my painting kit, broke the easel. I never touched her. I never had a chance, even if I'd wanted to."

Mom sat on the sand by me and reached a hand toward the cheek she'd slapped. She held it against me a moment and I put my hand on hers.

"She ranted about Doc and her sister. Most of it didn't make sense. She kept stumbling, feet catching on the rocks. She was wasted, Vince. And she kept edging closer to the cliff. I tried to warn her. I even screamed, but she was so out of control. When I stepped forward to grab her, to pull her back, she lurched away. She lost her balance, fell on the rocks and slipped over the edge. It happened so fast I couldn't believe it. Even as I watched her go, I couldn't believe it."

I squeezed her hand and then let it go.

"Why the charade about the suicide?"

"That was Dale's idea. He thought it would blow over if we said that. And she did kill herself—I just don't think that's what she intended. He was looking out for you, Vince."

"What about the money, Mom? How much was your silence worth?

"Five hundred thousand."

"Half a million? I hope you enjoyed it."

"No, Vince. It wasn't for us. We didn't want money; we only wanted you. We'd have paid her to adopt you. But she didn't understand that. In her mind, she could exert control over us through dollars. She created a trust, payable to you upon her death—provided that you never contacted the family and never pursued a claim. She thought your father and I would live up to the bargain so we could preserve that trust for you.

"In a way she was right," Mom continued. "Once you

reached eighteen, we figured that since we'd held off that long, a few more years wouldn't make a difference."

The old woman's words came back now: "That Indian didn't get a penny from us, and now I don't have to give you any, either." She'd set me up. That was why she'd met me that night.

"I wanted to tell you when your father was dying, but he wouldn't have it, Vince. He was afraid you'd remember him differently if you found out in his final days."

DEB SET A GLASS of water on the picnic table in front of me and wrapped my shoulders in a hug. I raised my face and blinked my eyes clear, still feeling like everything was happening in a haze.

We stood outside our back door. Mom sat on a boulder fifty yards closer to the beach, her knees drawn up and wrapped in her arms. The wind had cooled and shifted. It now blew from the north and raised goose bumps on my arms. I turned and put my head to Deb's neck, sank into her embrace, felt her fingers gliding up and down my back.

"How did you find out?" she asked.

"This morning the county clerk pulled the birth certificate of the child born the night of the accident. It was mine. I wasn't sure, because Mom and Dad—Loretta and Doc—were listed as the parents, not Autumn Coyote and William Pontcliff. But the coincidence was too much."

I paused and watched the growing waves curling toward us and breaking over the sand.

"Monty told me that back then adoptive parents could

request a new birth certificate from the county when an adoption when through. That way they could eliminate any reference to the biological parents. What I don't understand is why my parents celebrated my birthday in July but the birth record said October. They had to know I'd see it someday."

"Your mother told me that the day in July was when the adoption became official. Celebrating on the different day, I think that was her and your dad's way of letting you find out if something ever happened to them. They knew you'd question it."

"I guess."

"I'm sorry. I can't imagine what you're going through, Vince."

"I'm not going through much. I'm numb. And I'm angry at Vanessa Grey. I can't believe she'd sit right in front of me and not say anything. Instead she just set me up so she could break the trust. I walked right into her trap. Even in the end, she won."

"She didn't win, Vince."

"Right. She's dead and I'm alive. I have you and Glory and…and Mom. She was a bitter old woman who had no family. All that garbage will make me feel better next week or next month. But right now it doesn't. Right now all I can think about is that she died knowing that she drove one more stake through her son and through Autumn Coyote and through her grandson." I laughed. "It's funny, I still don't think of myself as that person, as her grandson. It's like I'm angry for what she did to someone else."

"She didn't win, Vince."

"Right," I grunted.

"That's what the letter said. The one you got in the mail. Vanessa Grey didn't win."

I pulled away from her. "What?"

"The letter from Helen. I gather she was Grey's nurse. She learned the truth. She explains it all in the letter. When she realized what had happened, that you were the child and that the Grey woman was going to revoke the trust…she wrote something about paying back a debt. The letter said she owed it to you because of what your father did for her."

"Dad saved her son. What did the letter say? She didn't…?"

"All she wrote was that Vanessa Grey didn't have a chance to revoke the trust before she, meaning Helen, took matters into her own hands. That's what she wrote: 'Took matters into my own hands.' She said you should consider it a favor returned."

EPILOGUE

Nine months later

"THE SIGN MUST BE somewhere near here," I said. "Mr. Stinson told me it was about three or four miles in."

I maneuvered the Bronco around a large, mud-filled hole in the old two-track. Deb rode next to me, Glory in the back. She kicked her foot against the back of my seat each time the vehicle bounced through a rut.

Until this week, snow and then spring runoff had made the road impassable. A low-riding car would still find travel difficult.

Sunlight glinted off the puddles and warmed the brown, dormant understory. In another month only stray beams would reach the ground, filtered through a green canopy overhead.

"There's a sign." Deb pointed toward a weathered plywood rectangle nailed to a large oak.

A rusted chain stretched from the oak to another massive tree, blocking an overgrown road. I pulled up near the chain and saw the faded name on the wood: STINSON.

"He said it's about a hundred yards in," I said.

We climbed out of the car. I swung Glory up onto my shoulders. She wrapped her little fingers into my hair and anchored them as we started down a grassy path. Low brush and alder saplings reached in toward us.

"I've been thinking more about daycare for Glory," I said. "What do you think about me staying home with her? You know, during the school year."

"You'd leave the *Chronicle?*"

"I think I could swing a deal with Lou to work from home, or maybe only part-time on evenings and weekends."

Deb reached up and held a low-hanging branch back so Glory could pass under.

"You'd have to commit to caring for her, Vince. You couldn't just plop her in front of the TV and write all day. And you couldn't run out every time the scanner went off, leaving her with various neighbors."

"I'd just bring her with me," I said, somewhat jokingingly. "I think we could afford it—now that the Grey family has decided to release the trust and all the accumulated earnings. Harlan Montgomery said things should clear the court in another week or two."

"I know it's not the money, Vince. It's just that reporting's been your life. Can you let it take a back seat to Glory?"

We walked further in silence, until the low trees opened into a clearing. A single-story log cabin filled the space. Sunlight, sparkling with dust motes, gave the cabin a dreamy glow.

Glory struggled free, and I lowered her to the dirt. She ran a few steps forward, squatted and examined something on the ground, a child's hidden treasure.

I grabbed Deb's hand. "You're right, Deb. Reporting has been my life. I want it to be something else for a while. I want to spend the time with our daughter, before she's old enough for school. I want to make up for lost days."

I squatted next to Glory and saw her studying a patch of trailing arbutus that had poked its delicate white flowers through the dead leaves.

"C'mon, Morning Glory, let's go find that trailer," I said.

She took the hand I offered and stood. Deb took my other hand, and together we strolled across the clearing, searching for my parents' cabin.

* * * * *